Starfish

The Arbitrary Ocean

Elizabeth Cooke

abbott press

This is a work of fiction. All of the characters, names, incidents, organizations, and dialogue
in this novel are either the products of the author's imagination or are used fictitiously.

Abbott Press books may be ordered through booksellers or by contacting:

Abbott Press
1663 Liberty Drive
Bloomington, IN 47403
www.abbottpress.com
Phone: 1 (866) 697-5310

ISBN: 978-1-4582-2124-7 (sc)
ISBN: 978-1-4582-2125-4 (hc)
ISBN: 978-1-4582-2123-0 (e)

Library of Congress Control Number: 2017911884

Print information available on the last page.

Abbott Press rev. date: 08/04/2017

PREAMBLE

Book One of The Rose Trilogy

VIOLET ROSE

THE ENCROACHING SEA

The book, "Violet Rose" begins in the 1950s and proceeds, as Violet Annas is born in 1962 in Westhampton Beach, Long Island. The little girl is haunted from the time she is six years old, by the vision of a terrible storm that pulled a house out to sea, with a family inside, and the sound of a child's cry. Forever, Violet feels part of the ocean she fears and worships.

The resort town where she lives with her family on Dune Road in a stilt house is beset by Nor'Easters and hurricanes that threaten to overrun Long Island itself. It is part of living a life on a shoreline subject to a sea that is changing with time, becoming more invasive as the planet warms.

20 years pass. Violet falls in love with a local policeman, Bud Rose, who has long been sleeping with another woman. Bud and Violet get married, much to the consternation of the rejected female, Jillian Burns. Her enmity and collusion with Violet's older brother, Sasha, who has long resented his sister, makes for a conspiracy against Violet and Bud that is as violent and overwhelming as are the tides of an unconstrained ocean.

Sasha is a brutal bully who has plagued his younger sister over the years. He is only too eager to destroy her happiness, as is Jillian, whose bitterness seeks a cruel revenge. Jillian's ultimate weapon against the married pair is the child of her lover, Bud Rose, she bears and names 'Rose Bud'.

The story starts in the 1950s when Westhampton Beach is a lazy resort town, the first 'Hampton' and the least chic; it continues into the 1980s when radical change due to the influx of wealth into the community brings local/visitor conflict; it ends in 1985, when life in Westhampton Beach is demonstrably different from 'the good old days' and the ocean threat is more intense.

The sea and its potential violence is the metaphor for a passionate love triangle that ends in violence.

The book, "Violet Rose" is only the beginning, as love, drama, and the arbitrary ocean itself sweeps over the world of Long Island and its inhabitants.

"STARFISH", The Arbitrary Ocean, is the second book in Elizabeth Cooke's The Rose Trilogy. It continues the life of Bud and Violet Rose, with the baby girl they call Starfish. As Assistant Deputy Sheriff of Suffolk County, Bud pursues a drug cartel that plagues the community. Much of the action takes place in Montauk, on the southeastern tip of Long Island, 'where the boats come in' with their supply not only of fish but the illegal substance called White Sugar. Throughout, the turbulent ocean mirrors the tumult in the lives of the characters.

Chapter One

ROSE

That terrible night, the 1ˢᵗ of May in 1985, the storm ROSE (so named by the weather service) hit the East End of Long Island. As Violet held in her arms, the illegitimate baby of her husband, Bud Rose, in a house in East Moriches, at that very moment, a gray Ford car driving fast on Dune Road, Westhampton Beach, flipped over, with the child's true mother and Violet's brother inside. Huge waves pulled the vehicle out to sea.

Violet looked at the sleeping child in her arms. There was a new, unrecognizable tug in her heart. Youngest in her family, Violet had never been around small children – much less babies. Even though this was not her own child but her husband Bud's, from an affair with Jillian Burns before Violet and he married, she determined to love the little child. And how could she not looking down into that face of innocence?

It was not until the next afternoon that Violet, Bud, and Stella Burns, the baby's grandmother, in whose house they were gathered, learned that Jillian Burns, mother of the child she called 'Rose Bud', and Sasha Annas were lost.

The three realized that the two had died in a terrible oceanic accident. With Violet's own brother, Sasha, driving the car, the automobile had been swept away by horrifying waves. The two were on the run from the police, having been identified as members of a car theft conspiracy that had plagued the East End of Long Island.

Ironically, Bud Rose, Sasha's brother-in-law and Violet's husband, had been chief detective on the case, so it was he who had received the report of the accident from his office at the Riverhead Police Department.

Bud and Violet had decided to stay the night at Stella Burn's house until the storm abated. They had come looking for Jillian who, had cut her ankle bracelet monitor, having been under house arrest. She was now long gone with Sasha in tow, and Bud, although conflicted about Rose Bud, had been genuinely concerned about the safety of his baby in the storm.

"Those two are on the lam," Bud had told Stella Burns when they had first arrived, dripping wet and beaten by wind. "It's a wonder we could get here through the storm."

Jillian's mother had seemed quite calm, but her words belied her demeanor. "I'm glad you made it. Frankly, I'm scared."

"How long have they been gone?" Bud had asked.

"Only an hour or two."

"You know your daughter is under suspicion," Bud had said, not unkindly. "Her ankle bracelet... Was it Sasha who cut it?"

"I guess so. He got some tools out of the garage." Stella Burns had then sat down bleakly on the couch in the living room.

"I'm afraid Jillian was up to her neck in trouble, Mrs. Burns. Maybe bad companions?"

"I'm not surprised," the older woman had responded. "Nothing about Jillian surprises me...except perhaps the good sense to have a man like you as father to her baby." Then, glancing at Violet. "Sorry my dear. Don't mean to offend, but you know, a good man is hard to find!"

Violet had shot her a wary glance.

Now, this late afternoon of mourning, they sat about the living room in the house in East Moriches. Stella Burns was in shock, her face pale and somber. Her daughter was gone.

As for Violet, she did not know what or how to feel. Sasha was mean, still Sasha was her brother, a deep part of her life. To die so young, as had Jillian! Tears filled her eyes as she reflected on hearing her mother, Anastasia's yelp of anguish over the phone, when she and Bud had called her earlier and told her the awful truth. And her father. His only son!

Now, Violet held the baby Rose Bud in her arms, as she sat next to Stella on the couch. Bud was sitting on a chair opposite the three females, watching them. In his sudden new life, this child, such a curious, unexpected little creature, had turned his world upside down. The little baby was from this moment on, his to raise, and his to love.

He got to his feet and announced, "Violet and I have got to return to Remsenburg soon, ladies, with Rose Bud…"

Violet remarked, "I cannot call her Rose Bud. I just can't!"

"Rosalina?" Stella suggested softly.

"No. Rosemary Rose? No. Rosewood Rose? No." Violet sighed. "I want to call her Starfish."

"You can't call her Starfish! Fish?" Stella's eyebrows shot up. "Fish?"

"No, of course not, but she is all golden in my arms, fresh from the sea." Violet thought of the golden starfish pin Bud had given her at their beginning, his first protestation of love. Starfish. Star. Then looking up, she said, "in Russian – you know, my mother was born in Russia – the word for morning star is 'aurora'. Perhaps Aurora Rose."

"Aurora. What a pretty name. My grandbaby girl, Aurora," exclaimed Stella, and for the first time, she bent her head and cried.

After further consoling Stella Burns on that grim afternoon, upon learning of the Jillian/Sasha drowning, Bud and Violet set out to return to their home in Remsenburg by Moriches Bay.

Before leaving, Bud assured Stella she would always be welcome "at our house. We're not far away and we will bring baby…Aurora, to you as often as you like. You will be a big part of her life. A little one always needs a grandma," he said with a grin.

"I'll miss her." Stella was sniffling into a linen handkerchief. "But it's only right she be with her father…and you, Violet."

"I'm certainly new at the game", Violet responded

"You'll be just fine," the older woman said. "Look how baby has already taken to you. There hasn't been a peep out of her since you took her up."

In his cruiser car, the young policeman/detective had packed the few tiny garments belonging to his baby, Rose Bud, – newly named, Aurora – plus, a canvas bag with a quantity of diapers, talcum powder, Vaseline, Q-tips –several bottles of baby milk formula – necessities for the little one – as well as his and Violet's overnight case. They also took the basket/bassinet, provided by Stella, which Violet cradled in her arms, baby inside in her blankets, all the way home.

Of course, Aurora, being only five months old was quite oblivious to these machinations and managed to sleep her way to her new home. "Aurora," Violet whispered. "My little morning star...fish." Violet thought, 'to me she will always be Starfish – tossed up from the ocean waves – saved because she was not in that cursed car that went into the deep – a child's cry now quiet because she is safe in my arms.'

On the drive, which was hazardous, although the storm was long past, the sun was shining eerily from a foggy sky. As they passed close to the ocean, the surface of the sea frothed a mossy-green. Calmer now, the waves looked dream-like, in a glowing haze, as if sated, satisfied after their destructive outburst.

Chapter Two

RESURFACE

"Christ, Sasha! Are you really trying to kill us?"

These had been the last words Jillian shrieked, that fateful night, that 1st of May, 1985, as the violent storm, ROSE, hit the eastern end of Long Island. The gray Ford Sasha was driving flipped over into the huge wave as it roared in, covering Dune Road, just as the car had turned towards Hampton Bays.

Sasha had already opened the front door on the driver's side, as he saw the water towering. He had grabbed Jillian, and with a strength enhanced by adrenaline, he managed to drag her from the front seat, her long legs kicking against the water.

With his right hand, Sasha, with the luck of a God he did not even respect, grasped ahold of the base of the guardrail that circled the curve on Dune Road. Pulling Jillian next to him, she too was able to clutch the low metal railing with both hands. The two clung together there, inching forward, each time the waves receded until they were literally wrapped around the metal piece that saved their unruly lives.

What an incredible night! Half drowned, the two held on for dear life. They did not speak. The only sound – other than the roar of wind and crash of water – was that of a gurgling throat (Jillian), and water spat onto the road (Sasha).

But they survived. They were alive. As morning light began to filter dimly through the cloudy atmosphere, as the rain abated and the wind cooled down, the two trusted enough to untangle themselves from the railing and attempt to set foot on the muddy, sodden road.

They were able to walk with a stagger, clutching one another, in the direction of Hampton Bays, the town to the north of Dune Road. More than once, Jillian slipped to the ground, much to the disgust of her companion.

"Get up, Jillian. For Christ's sake, are you such a pussy? I thought you were tough." Sasha's bullyboy personality was on show under the stress of the situation. "For Christ's sake. Do I have to leave you here in the mud?"

"Please, Sasha," she could only breathe, but his words spurred her to extra effort and she managed to continue the torturous journey.

It continued this way for many minutes. Finally, as a sliver of sunshine broke through the heavens, Sasha exclaimed, "Hey look. There's what seems to be a broken-down garage over there on that patch of ground, on the left!" And indeed, there was a door-less, small building, half atilt. It looked like it had been hit by a truck – but no, Jillian thought, 'Hit by a wall of water!'

"At least it's got a roof," Sasha muttered. "Nobody will see us. Come on!"

And they made their way through the mushy, sloshy grass, over bits of lumber and broken boards to the tilted building with its filthy floor and shattered garage door on the ground at the entrance.

"At least it's dryer inside!" Sasha said, giving Jillian a forceful shove into the small building.

Jillian had had the foresight to keep the shoulder strap of her purse (with cash amounting to a little over $300, plus makeup and credit cards) tight across her body, as the waves hit. Of course, everything inside her purse, - a flowered kerchief, a pair of sunglasses - as well as every bit of clothing on her, was soaked with seawater, briny with salt.

"When the sun really comes out, I can at least dry the bills," she said, brushing back her wet hair.

"Bills? What bills?"

"My money, Sasha, what there is of it. The credit cards too. They're plastic so, wiping them dry should be easy…"

"Are you crazy! Credit Cards! Jillian, we're dead! No way can we use credit cards."

"Dead?"

"Dead! That's right, Jillian," he shouted. "We no longer exist. There is no Sasha Annas! There is no Jillian Burns!"

Tears coursed down the face of the leggy brunette, in her sopping clothes, sitting on the concrete floor of a blown-out garage on the edge of Hampton Bays.

Dead! Jillian's thoughts overwhelmed her. Dead! She saw only a vacuum ahead. The world she knew was over. There was no past. Jillian Burns did not exist. Perhaps she never had. The tears flowed. It was May 1st, 1985. A new world and a whole new life had to be created…and a lying life to be lived

Chapter Three

THE SUN CAME OUT — AND THE MONEY

"I'm hungry." Jillian remarked as she recovered herself, wiped the tears with the back of her hand, and tried to get her bearings in the garage. "I'm famished."

"Aw, quit your grousing. We're breathing! Nothing's broken! We're okay, aren't we? The sun's in the sky. The wind has gone. For God's sake, count your blessings."

Sasha was busily removing his sodden jacket, then the wet shirt beneath. Jillian watched in fascination as he started to peel off the plastic wrap about his upper torso, revealing numbers of $100 bills, one after the other. He carefully placed each one on the floor at his feet, crouching there, concentrated.

"God, Sasha! How much do you have?"

"A lot," he grunted.

And there were a lot, for he had stacked them carefully, overlapping, all the way down to his crotch. Of course, the bills were wet, but not as soaked as his clothes, and the main thing was, they were intact and quite perfect.

Jillian gazed open-mouthed at this performance. It prompted her to reach for her purse and lay out her own bills – mostly $20s – amounting to $280 in all – except for a number of $5s and $1s. She laid them in the sun, flat on the concrete at the entrance of the building and waited patiently until she could collect them in a neat little dry pile next to her. This task was executed with absolutely no conversation. The only sound was the slight swish of paper as bills were assigned to a sunny spot.

Their efforts completed, as the sun grew high in the sky, Jillian asked "What time is it? Is your watch working?"

"Yep," he said. "It's close to 2:00 o'clock."

"We need some food. I feel faint."

"There you go again...Miss Tough Girl. But you're right. We need sustenance."

Sasha remembered that there was a 7-Eleven store not far, up on West Montauk Highway, a road that ran through the center of the town of Hampton Bays. He figured that he could walk up there, grab some food and return to Jillian, because he too was really hungry.

"Give me those small bills and maybe a $20," he said to his companion who was sitting disconsolately at the garage entrance, fluffing her dark hair in the sun.

"Here! Take what you want. And get some water. I'm dying of thirst. Be sure you come back!" she added.

"You're kidding" Sasha replied, eying his pile of cash left in her care. He pulled his still damp jacket about him and grabbed her small bills. "I'll be quick. When I return, we have to do some major planning. – new names – where to land – how to stay dead!" And with those unsettling final words, he placed dark glasses on his nose and took off, heading toward Hampton Bays.

'Dead,' she thought. 'Dead! I don't exist.'

She was not sure how long it was before Sasha returned. She had been sitting there at the front of the garage in a kind of trance, watching the road and the bridge that crossed the Shinnecock Inlet, looking for movement, but the life outside was still. No person emerged. The sun was growing hot. There was no wind. It was if the world had stopped.

For her it had. For Sasha it had, Jillian thought, when she finally heard his footsteps first, then Sasha appeared with a large paper bag of things to eat. Suddenly, her hunger for food and for life itself arose in such force, she blurted, "At last. What did you get? And water? You have water?"

"Yes, yes. Hold your horses. Let me set this down. Stop clawing at me." He handed her a bottled water.

Jillian quickly drank the whole down. "Whew! I needed that. What'd you get to eat?"

"Well, 7-Eleven was pretty empty – not only of customers but of food. They've had no deliveries of fresh stuff for the last two days – but I got a box of Entenmann's Donuts – shouldn't be too stale..."

"Donuts? That's all?"

"No. Don't be so impatient. There were no salads or hot dishes, but there were a couple of leftover sandwiches." Sasha presented Jillian with a ham and cheese on rye wrapped in plastic. "Oh, and I got a banana."

Jillian was busy unwrapping the sandwich from its casing. All she could think of was Sasha releasing the $100 bills from their plastic imprisonment on his chest earlier that morning. She devoured the food in seconds, and mouth full, asked Sasha, "Banana?"

"Jeez!" he exclaimed and handed her the fruit with its darkening yellow skin.

"Some meal," Jillian growled unhappily.

Sasha crouched down beside her, his figure menacing. "Listen, you. What in hell do you expect! There's been a storm that's probably killed a few people – that almost killed us, for God's sake. The power is still out! Lots of buildings are badly damaged. Trees are in the roads, knocked down with dangerous power lines wrapped around them – and you come off, griping like a spoiled brat."

Jillian blanched. She said nothing.

"From now on, shape up or I swear you'll be on your own. I'll be off and running because I intend to survive and not go to prison. If that's your future, Jillian Burns, good luck, but I'm not hanging around to find out."

He got to his feet and went to the edge of the garage. His back was to her. She rose and coming from behind, put her arms around him and pressed into his back.

"I've been stupid and I'm sorry and I'm scared."

10

"Well, get over it – the scared part," he said turning to her. "We have to create two new identities - new names – and we'll play the married couple for the world." He patted her shoulder. "Do you have anything with you that has your initials?"

She shook her head.

"Who do you want to be?"

"Jillian Burns." Her voice was low.

"Now you ARE being stupid."

"I was trying to make a joke."

"Seriously, Jillian. What's a name you've always wanted?"

She thought a moment. "I've always loved the name Scarlet. Mom took me to see 'Gone With The Wind' when I was about 10 at the Westhampton Beach Theater – it was winter and they had an old-movie club. Yeah. Scarlet. Hey, I could dye my hair red!"

"Now you're thinking! And I? I've always wanted to be an Englishman. How about Alistair? Just call me Al." Sasha laughed. "I could grow a moustache. Not a beard – but a pencil-thin moustache! I like it. Alistair and Scarlet Williams – from Teaneck New Jersey."

"Well, how do you do!" Jillian said. She began to enjoy this new game they were to play and the challenges ahead. "Scarlet Williams, red-head from Teaneck – have you ever been to Teaneck?" she asked him. Now she was laughing with the thought. "I know I haven't, but who cares. Alistair and Scarlet Williams have just come to town – but which town? Hampton Bays? Southampton?"

"How about Montauk?"

"Montauk!" Sasha nodded his head. "Nobody would think to look for us there."

"I went there once - as a kid – to see the lighthouse on Montauk Point. Montauk itself is a nice little town – touristy in summer. Somehow we could get lost there." Jillian was growing excited about this new adventure.

"Montauk!" Sasha exclaimed. "It works for me."

The two gathered themselves together, Sasha – now Alistair -putting his cash in the paper bag that had carried the food, and Jillian – now Scarlet – putting on the semidry flowered kerchief over her hair, donning the Jackie O. type sunglasses, round, large and dark. "Hey Al," she called to him. " How do I look? Just wait 'til I can dye my hair."

They walked in the sunlight to the Hampton Bays Railroad Station – Montauk Branch, at the intersection of Springville Road and Goodground Road, just east of Ponquogue Avenue, and south of the main drag of Hampton Bays.

The two seated themselves on a bench under an eave in the old station house, out of the sun, and finished off the water Sasha/Alistair – had bought and waited for a train. They would buy their tickets on board.

"Do you think the trains are running?" Jillian/Scarlet asked forlornly.

"I do. That's the first thing the county clears, after a storm, the railroad tracks. From New York City all the way out."

"I hope you're right!" Jillian/Scarlet said.

He held his tongue but glared at his companion. "We should get there in maybe an hour, I would think," he said finally. "Montauk's only about 30 or 40 miles east of us."

"Sure...once a train comes," she remarked sarcastically. "The first thing to do is go to a drug store and get some hair dye."

"Then an out of the way motel. Fortunately 'the season' hasn't started yet. Shouldn't be a problem."

Near 4:30 pm, an old man wandered down the platform, the only other passenger for a train that was just pulling into the station, heading east. And with a toot and whistle, Alistair and Scarlet Williams from Teaneck New Jersey, were on their way to creating a whole new world.

Chapter Four

RORI

"Rori. I'm going to call her Rori," Bud was saying as they turned into the driveway of their house on Shore Road in Remsenburg. "Aurora is just too formal for a little baby."

"You can call her whatever you like, Mr. Cop, but I'm calling her Starfish," Violet said with a smile. As she looked through the car's front window, she let out a little cry. "My God. The house!"

Before them, their home had taken major blows. In fact, the driveway itself was blocked, so the two, with Bud carrying the basket/bassinet, had to proceed on foot to the entrance. There were sticks and shattered planks of wood from unknown sources that lay before them that they were forced to clamber over.

"Thank God the roof's in one piece," Bud exclaimed.

Fortunately, there had never been big trees near the house, only scrubby reed-like bushes. These had been ripped apart and were scattered close to the front stoop. Violet had to climb over the branches as she put the key in the lock to open the door, the top half of which was made of glass. The glass was not there. It was gone and smashed at her feet.

She managed to push the door open. Much of the interior furniture in the living room had moved. There was a chair up against the front door that she shoved aside. But surprisingly, although things were in disarray, the floor was dry. There was no water damage.

"It's those eight-foot stanchions we put under the house, kept us high and dry," Bud said as he entered behind his wife.

Violet was standing in the middle of the room. "Was there a window open? How did everything get pushed around?"

"I guess the house shook," Bud said sinking onto the couch, which was straddled across the door to the bedroom. "Do you suppose the TV still works?" he asked, placing the bassinet/basket down. The TV, which had been on a table, was now in the middle of the floor. Bud picked it up and replaced it, pushing the table against the outer wall and plugging it in.

The screen came on immediately with a local news program where the weather girl was describing the past hours and what was to come. "Nothing but sunny days ahead," she chirped, as Bud's voice, suddenly loud and clear exclaimed, "Oh God! Our deck is gone."

The two rushed to the window, and sure enough, there was nothing left of the two wicker chairs, the little table where they placed their wine glasses and watched the golden sunsets, the deck itself, now in bits and pieces on the reeds below.

"It can be fixed," Violet said dolefully, as she turned on hearing the baby's cry.

In the beginning, through those first days of step-motherhood, Violet made her way, at first tentatively, then with more assurance. She set up a changing table and the bassinet in the large walk-in closet next to the bedroom. With the door open, she was available to hear every breath that little Rori/Starfish took.

There was a rocking chair already near the bedroom window where Violet was able to feed the baby. 'Thank God for bottled baby milk,' she thought, laughing to herself. 'That would have been a problem.'

She had called Bethany at Brandeis Realty, saying she'd have to make child-care arrangements before she could come back to work.

"Of course, sweetheart. I understand. I heard about the accident." She paused. "So you've taken that awful woman's baby under your wing?"

Violet bristled. "Look, Bethany. She's Bud's flesh and blood - a sweet little thing – poor little girl. Of course I'll 'take her under my wing', as you put it. I intend to raise her as my own."

"Well, don't get so exercised! I admire you for being able to do that, Violet. Not a lot of young women in your position would." She paused, then, "Anyway, take your time. You know you're always welcome here. In fact you're needed." She paused again. "Hey, do you know what's happened to your Dad's house in the storm – out there on the dunes?"

"Oh, it's still there!" Violet said coldly, emphatically. Bethany Brandeis had wanted the listing on that house of her father's – the little dune house on stilts that he had lived in since the 1950s, where Violet had grown up. Bethany salivated over getting the listing because of the location of Mr. Annas' home – right next to The Swordfish Club – the center of beach activity. The plot he was on was worth a fortune, the house a pittance – so easy to tear down and build a seashore mansion – like the one next door. Bethany Brandeis could taste the deal.

"Take care of yourself and the baby, Violet. What's her name?"

"Her name is Aurora – but Bud calls her Rori. I call her Starfish."

"Starfish? Well, I guess that's better than Rose Bud! Isn't that what that Jillian woman called her? Rose Bud Rose!" Bethany laughed. "Rori Rose. Now that's pretty cute. But Starfish Rose?"

Violet laughed and hung up the phone, disgruntled. "Pretty cute indeed." She went to pick up the baby who was chortling in the playpen Violet had placed in the living room.

"Rori. My little star. My Starfish. You're safe now, baby. And you're mine."

Later that May of 1985, Detective Bud Rose was given a promotion. He was made a Deputy Sheriff of Suffolk County. His office was now in the Suffolk County Sheriff's Office, the oldest branch of law enforcement in the county, situated in the Riverhead Correctional Facility at 100 Center Street South – an address that was really in Riverside, - not Riverhead, but just south of the Peconic River in the Town of Southampton.

As a Deputy Sheriff, of which there were several, Bud's pay was higher. His duties covered all of Suffolk County, the easternmost county in Long Island, over 900 miles in size, and went all the way to Montauk Point on the tip of the South Fork and to Orient Point on the North Fork.

Bud had a new car, with his title on the side of the vehicle in large letters.

Since Bud's almost single-handedly cracking the expensive automobile case earlier in the year, his reputation and value had risen in the community. So Deputy Sheriff's position was only to be expected.

After all, the New Yorker, Vinny Rocco, arranger of the thefts from the driveways along the gilded coast, was incarcerated and facing10 years in Federal prison. His cohorts and actual robbers of said cars were Tad and Willie Yablonski – who turned out to be brothers. Each were expected to do less serious – but sizeable – jail time, as well. Jillian Burns, driver and deliverer of those vehicles off the ferry into New London hands, and Sasha, Bud's own brother-in-law and equal culprit – he and Jillian had been lost to the sea in a violent storm…

(Or so the world on the East End of Long Island believed).

Chapter Five

SCARLET WOMAN

Scarlet Williams was a different woman. Jillian Burns cut her hair short in a pixie cut with a pair of nail scissors. She dyed it a bright, red. And she chose mauve lipgloss and polish for her nails.

In the past, she had regularly worn business clothes – suits – loose jackets – even white, men's shirts with her jeans - as she had worked in the Sheriff's Office in Westhampton Beach, and later, as receptionist at the Storage Warehouse out near the Suffolk County Air Base. For dress up, it was always long flowered skirts and loose blouses.

Not any more. The jeans she wore were cut-offs, and at the end of her long legs, she sported short, high-heeled boots. The blouses she wore were off-shoulder and tight, and she fancied a white or black bow tie sitting brightly around her throat above the bare skin of her cleavage. Yes indeed! Scarlet Williams, Mrs. Alistair Williams, was a totally different kettle of fish.

And as for her quasi husband, happy Al Williams, with his thin dark moustache, well, he too made Sasha Annas disappear, with the cut of his jib, his English ascot and tweed jacket – even in summer – and the smart, white well-cut trousers. He looked ready to go to his club and smoke a cigar over a sloe gin.

Of course, the two had to earn a living. Money was still there in the paper bag in the closet in the small bedroom of the cabin they found at The Bayview of Hither Hills State Park. The rent was cheap because the establishment had originally been an old tourist cabin site, now updated.

The Williams couple was able to obtain a cabin surrounded by woods, for the price of $600 per month. There, they were able to hide out in a belligerent unmarried state.

Both had managed to find jobs appropriate to their appearances. Alistair, with his foppish British air found a job at the upscale Montauk Yacht Club on Star Island in the middle of Montauk Lake. It was a coup, but the place was hiring for the summer influx and found happy Al a good fit to oversee the dining room.

Sasha/Alistair had thrown himself into the interview with the Yacht Club's Director with great enthusiasm – and even a bit of poignancy, as he explained how he and his wife had lost everything in the recent storm, ROSE, his papers, his credit cards, even his driver's license (untrue). He was a good talker and in spite of his rather brutal personality, Sasha/Alistair had a certain charm and a way with words when he needed them.

In any case, he got the job, partly because he presented a combination of the proper Brit and the glad hand American, 'Call me Al'.

The pay was decent. With the 'paper-bag' leftover cash, he was able to buy a secondhand car, an old Chevy, dark green, from an aging fisherman who needed the couple of thousand dollars for medical purposes. Although the interior smelled intensely of the sea and its occupants, Alistair managed – with sprays of scented air-spray - to tamp it down.

Now, Jillian/Scarlet, again, because the hamlet of Montauk, residential population a little over 3000 souls, was preparing for the tourist crowd that came every summer, quickly found a job as well. The town, consisting of small businesses that served its people, a large fishing community – both commercial and recreational – and the park keepers and rangers who tended to the numerous nearby state parks, prepared to be inundated.

Montauk and the Lighthouse at Montauk Point, the fishing enclaves, the trails in the woods and on the dunes, brought visitors from all over the world to the area in the warm months.

So the town was gearing up, when Scarlet Williams walked into Joe's Warm-Up Bar off Main Street, and Joe himself met the tall redhead in her miniskirt and white leather boots. He was impressed. It was not only her looks. Scarlet was intelligent, not ditzy at all. And she seemed put together and competent. (She was.)

Also, there was a boldness Joe appreciated. A woman needed that in a raucous bar on a lively Saturday night, and she was thin enough to get between the extra tables he placed around the barroom during the summer months to take in the extra people who were ready to party.

"I'll start you out bringing drinks and bussing tables. You may get some good tips. Also, I think I'll teach you to bartend. You can talk a good game. (She could.) "And, well, your looks are… an attraction."

Scarlet smiled. "The pay?"

"It's by the hour, but more than minimum wage. $9:00."

"Make it $10 and you've got yourself a waitress slash bar maid," Scarlet said with her most seductive smile and wink.

"Okay. Okay. It's a deal. Can you start Saturday?"

She just nodded, turned and with a sly glance over her shoulder, said, "Bye bye, Joe Warm-Up. See you Saturday around 5:00," at which she heard him chuckle.

It wasn't much – the money. But Scarlet knew it was only the beginning. Joe Warm-Up might just possibly be her latest prey. Because a prey she needed. The rancor in her heart against Bud Rose had diminished not one jot, and hatred has to go somewhere. Why not against the 52 year-old bar owner? Playing with him could amuse her for a while, and deflect the venom in her heart, appease it for a moment.

Violet, too was in Jillian/Scarlet's line of fire. There would come a day when true vengeance against Bud and Violet would be hers. The anger in her had hardened to a tight mass. Bud had left her alone, pregnant – even if he didn't know she was. The loss of him had devastated Jillian/Scarlet – and to marry that blonde cupcake! That was the kiss of death.

Vengeance! 'I don't know how. I don't know when. But that it happens, I have not a doubt'.

As for the baby girl, Rose Bud? Scarlet did not give her a thought.

Chapter Six

A 1985 SUMMER IN THE HAMPTONS

Back in Remsenburg, Bud had called a construction friend and the small deck off the living room of the house on Shore Road was replaced in a matter of days. The evening it was completed, Bud and Violet, with baby Aurora –Rori – Starfish - sat on a wicker sofa, facing Moriches Bay and in the distance, Dune Road.

They watched as the sun went down, casting streaks of gold across quiet waters. On other evenings, sometimes, darker rays on the waves, as they crested, seemed to spring from beneath, troubled and uncompromising.

On each quiet end of day, as they enjoyed their Pinot Noir, the baby chortled and wheezed and cried and smiled. She was dimpled with a bit of fuzzy hair at the top of her head, and both Bud and Violet were quite in love with the little child. He was in awe of Violet's response to this illegitimate creation he had produced with the now dead Jillian. The breadth of Violet's heart amazed him. And he was grateful.

Violet had returned to work at the realty office. Bethany grew to depend on her and allowed the baby to come to work too. Violet was promoted - no longer receptionist - now agent. A young man named Henry Wilkes took over the front desk. Violet was given a small office at the back of the Brandeis Realty building. Next to it was a storage room with space for a playpen, a small changing table and mini-fridge.

"What a good little one," Bethany exclaimed. The infant was a quiet, sleepy, serene little girl, and the realtor, having never had children, was both intrigued and a bit intimidated by her. "Does she keep you up at night? I've heard babies can be quite fitful..."

"No, no," was Violet's reply. "She's incredibly good."

"You're a grand mother, Violet. And I really love having her here," and Bethany went over and knelt down, in her smart, gray suit next to the playpen. "Hi, baby," she cooed. "Hi, sweet little girl."

Rising with a sigh, Bethany changed personality to her business-self. "Let's get to work, my dear. There's an Open House scheduled for next Sunday – that big listing on Dune Road – the old mansion way up at the top of a dune – you know, it used to be the Fritchie's place – now Silverstein. He bought it only last year but wants to sell – at a much-inflated price, I'm sorry to say."

"Silverstein's flipping it?"

"You could say so," Bethany said with a laugh. She sat down before Violet's desk. "Can you handle it next Sunday... you know, with baby and all? I mean, she can't be with you at that house."

"No problem. My mother loves to baby sit."

"Good. That's settled." Bethany sat for a moment.

"Is there something else?" Violet asked. "You look like you've got something on your mind."

"Very perceptive, my dear. I do indeed have something I'm considering – which would mean large changes for me – and for you."

"What sort of changes?"

"I'm thinking of opening another office. We have four licensed agents here – other than you – and of course the new guy, Henry, makes five– and then of course there's me." Bethany paused. "Brandeis Realty made a lot of money this year...twice what we did last year. The East End of Long Island is hot!"

Bethany got to her feet. "I'm considering an office farther east ..."

"Southampton? Really?" Violet questioned.

"No way! That's a locked up town for a new realtor. No, no, much farther east. I'm thinking of Montauk."

"Montauk!"

"Yes. As yet it's untapped, but I guarantee in the next years, it will be a bonanza," Bethany said, her enthusiasm rising. Enthusiasm. It was what made her such a great saleswoman. She continued, "Montauk is a fascinating historical area. It's an idyllic community with of course fabulous beaches – world-renowned sport fishing – and the biggest fishing fleet in the country. It has state parks for hiking…"

"And Montauk Point Lighthouse!"

"And there's the radar tower over at Camp Hero and the air force base…anyway, I could go on and on. Why, Teddy Roosevelt had a place there …" Bethany stopped speaking. She stood up. Then, with a clap of her hands she exclaimed, "Enough already. That town – Montauk – Here I come!"

Chapter Seven

BRANDEIS BRANCH

Good to her word, that spring of 1985, Bethany's decision to expand the business became a reality. She was making a bundle, in Westhampton Beach, so she felt it time to enrich herself further and establish a second office to take advantage of the growing popularity of the East End.

She knew a Southampton location was out of the question. The Real Estate establishments there – of which there were two competing companies – were cutthroat and indomitable. She had decided to go farther east, to the hamlet of Montauk, the incomparable fishing village and resort, as yet quite undiscovered in terms of properties for sale or summer rentals. People would go down there for the beaches and the day fishing boat excursions and for the State Parks– and of course for the Lighthouse at the tip of Montauk Point. But for permanent summer residence – for a house by the sea - the market was as yet untapped.

Bethany intended to make that market her own. Born and raised in North Carolina, this lady had a southern charm all her own – and even a bit of a leftover southern accent. When enthused about a special piece of property, she would exclaim, "It's out of this worl'!" (No 'd').

She was still trying to list George Annas' stilt house on Dune Road, Westhampton Beach, because the building was on land that was truly 'Out of this worl'!' in terms of value…truly big bucks… so far, no success. 'The man is so stubborn," was her opinion of George Annas, Violet's father.

One late May morning, Bethany jumped into her car, a white Lexus, and headed east. She wore a perfectly tailored white pants suit with a pale gray and white silk scarf at her throat. Bethany was clothes conscious and always impeccably dressed, her small figure – her pride and joy - shown off to its best advantage.

She drove through Southampton, stopping for lunch at Sant Ambroeus, on N. Main Street, an Italian place, known for its gelatos and sherbets. There, she sat at a booth table in the restaurant area at the back, and devoured the ricotta stuffed ravioli in a brown butter sauce with sage leaves. It was an indulgence she craved.

Continuing on, through Easthampton and Napeague, she finally reached Montauk, the small village with a number of shops along Main Street. The Carl Fisher Office Building dominated the landscape, the tallest structure in the area, built in the 1930s in Tudor Style. It looked out of place in this basic fishing village. Tastes were changing, and Montauk had begun to attract visitors and tourists who wished to stay longer than just a day trip. People came in trailers to the State Parks and to the Point, but soon enough, true houses would be in demand.

"It's time they come to stay for real," Bethany muttered to herself as she parked the Lexus on Main Street and entered a law office that centered the line of small shops.

She had an appointment. Her own lawyer for the Brandeis Realty Company she owned, Mel Haddock, had contacted Attorney Augustus Brandt in Montauk and set up the meeting for 3:00 PM. She was right on time.

She entered through the glass door and announced herself to the receptionist. Within minutes, Mr. Brandt appeared and seemed delighted to usher such a pretty woman into his inner office. He was a tall man, of early middle age, in good shape, with black-rimmed glasses on the tip of his nose.

"I understand you want to open a Real Estate branch here in Montauk, is that right? Mel indicated to me that was your intent," he said in his most lawyerly tone.

"Indeed I do," Bethany replied. "Brandeis Realty is doing extremely well in Westhampton Beach, of course, and the surrounding area – Remsenburg, Quogue, Quiogue,– even as far east as Hampton Bays. I feel it's time to expand." She gave the lawyer her best smile.

"But so far east? What about Southampton and Easthampton?'

"Both towns have formidable Real Estate offices already established. As yet, Montauk seems a bit behind the curve, as they say. I would like to have the first foot in the door."

"You have a point, Miss Brandeis."

"Oh, please call me Bethany."

"Bethany," he said, his face reddening. "And call me Gus."

"Are there any available locations I might look at?"

"There are three I can show you. In fact, I already arranged to see them – have the keys," and he reached in the top drawer of his desk and retrieved them, then stood up. "Now?" he questioned.

"Of course. That's wonderful," and with that, the two left his office. Gus led her down the street.

The first shop front was right there on Main Street. It was small, with only one back office area.

"Out of the question," Bethany said, disappointed.

The second venue on Old Montauk Highway – (they took Bethany's car) - was larger, but the condition of the space would require a lot of refurbishing. "It looks quite decrepit," Bethany said.

"Yes, but the location is great and the price is right."

It was the third listing they looked at that fit the bill, a small building, by itself, set on a patch of grass. On The Circle, in the downtown section of the southwest corner of Old Montauk Highway, the structure had three good-sized office rooms at the rear, a welcoming reception area up front, and the place was in relatively good condition. In fact, it could be used 'as is' to start. Adornments could be added later, along with a fresh paint job.

"Yes, oh yes," Bethany said happily. "This is going to be perfect."

"It's not cheap," Gus said to her. "The rent..."

"Rent? No, no. I want to buy."

"You want to buy it?"

"Yes. It is for sale, no?"

"Well, yes...it is."

"Well, let's do it, Gus. I mean it."

"Don't you want to know the price?"

"Let's go back to your office."

And they did, and she did, and Bethany Brandeis Realty was now the prospective new owner of a small building on The Circle in Montauk, Long Island, N.Y.

It was growing dark by the time intent papers were signed and a check proffered as deposit. Bethany was delighted. So was Gus Brandt. "Come on. We have to celebrate," he exclaimed. "Right near your new property is one of the oldest taverns on Long Island. It's on the Highway – just a stone's throw from your new purchase…called Shagwong's…"

"What an odd name!"

He laughed. "Well, yeah, but it's been around for a long while – lots of crusty old fishermen go there, but also, people like me as well - pretty damned good seafood and cold, cold beer. The soft-shell crab sandwich is famous – and worth every bite. How about it? Don't you deserve to know where you're likely to have lunch or dinner when you're in business?" This was said with a tilt of his head and a provocative smile.

"When you put it that way, Gus, how can I resist," Bethany replied with a toss of her shoulder-length dark blond hair, one of her crowning glories. The flirtation was on!

And they were off to a delightful evening with Tequila Sunrise cocktails, fresh, raw clams and that delectable soft-shell crab sandwich.

Live music – a guitar and piano, played at the end of the bar. Bethany couldn't help but be appalled by the large shark snout with its spear sticking out into the room, but it only added to the rustic atmosphere.

Bethany was elated with her purchase, elated with Montauk, even elated with Gus Brandt. The closing on the building was set for the following week. She had put down some real money, and the deal was well on its way to completion.

She could see herself in that building She could see herself here at Shagwong's, lunching or dining with many a new client, and she could almost see herself in the arms of Gus Brandt. And to him? She was already there. Why he could even taste her!

Chapter Eight

THE MONTAUK YACHT CLUB

It was an elegant place Alistair had found for employment, and this delighted him. He could play the best British version of himself, suave and sure, with his new thin moustache. He worked the dining room as host, and soon enough, took on the position of *sommelier*, with a pay increase of almost one-third, during that summer of 1985

Set on Star Island in the middle of Montauk Lake, really a saltwater bay, the sunsets viewed from the outer deck of The Montauk Yacht Club, which had fire pits, lit in the early evening, were spectacular. The golden-streaked sky, the fire red in the pits made for sensational spectacle.

At the entrance of the club was a replica of the Montauk Point Lighthouse. There was a poolside bar, plus, inside, the Gulf Coast Kitchen, the main dining room. Although casual, it presented bright blue glasses and yellow napkins. Famous for its seafood – the mussels in white wine, the lobster in butter sauce, the stuffed flounder - the menu was eclectic and of the freshest.

And the wines! They were top of the line. Alistair did his homework. He was nothing if not a hard worker and he became familiar with the vintage bottles of the Montauk Yacht Club cellar.

Not unlike Scarlet/Jillian, Alistair/Sasha – he too – harbored an abiding hatred for Bud Rose and Violet, his own sister. In the first place, Bud had been the leading detective and closer in the car robberies case. Alistair did not consider them crimes – merely a strategy to get money – and it had worked well for a time. He had reaped thousands of dollars –some of which were still in the paper bag in the closet at the cabin.

Alistair hated Bud because he had closed the lucrative business down and caused him to run and hide – and this hiding place – this Montauk Yacht Club – in fact, was not a bad place to stay undercover. But it rankled him to have to play such a game, to have to hide in plain sight.

Sasha/Alistair had been Bud Rose's Best Man in his wedding to Violet. Alistair did not find him a bad guy – except for the fact that he had married his sainted sister who Sasha despised. She had always been his father's favorite, had always gotten the attention Sasha felt he deserved. And for what? Because she was pretty? Because she was a girl?

So he, along with Jillian/Scarlet awaited a revenge he knew would come.

"It ain't over 'til the fat lady sings," he muttered to himself. "And she'll be singing soon!"

The warm summer moved in on Long Island, busy with tourists and summer residents. Before 'the fat lady did any singing', there came a moment that threatened Alistair's ersatz world.

It was a gorgeous July evening. Alistair was presiding at the head desk in the dining room, checking reservations with the gentry who were arriving for dinner. Many had been outside on the fire-pit deck, enjoying the view over a dry martini or gin and tonic and were fairly into their cups when they presented themselves to Alistair. This did not bother him at all.

"By the window, Al," one regular requested.

"I'll see that you get a window table, Mr. Reynolds," and Alistair beckoned a waiter over to escort the Reynolds couple. As they walked away, Mr. Reynolds said, with a wink, "and come over later. We'll want a special wine."

Alistair noted that the long married Mr. Reynolds was with a very hot looking young woman, young enough to be his daughter –only he didn't have a daughter. 'Ah well,' he thought. 'I guess it's not unusual at The Montauk Yacht Club. Not unusual at all,' and he smiled to himself.

The smile quickly faded when he saw the next couple as they approached the front desk! He grew pale and nervous. Would they recognize Sasha Annas/Alistair Williams?

Earlier in the week, Jordan Mather had decided to bring wife Janice, an aging but still lovely looking blonde woman, for a weekend away from the house in Quogue on Dune Road. The large place was full of their adult kids – with their girl friends in bikinis, ready for the beach, which was directly across from the Mather mansion on Dune Road.

Janice had had her fill of her husband's ogling of the young girls. She had grown petulant and determined to remove him from temptation – she was not uninformed about her husband's peccadillos – so it was her suggestion they get away for a few days alone and "leave the young ones to play unobserved."

He agreed. On a Thursday evening, the Mathers had driven down from Quogue, not at all an onerous journey. They were staying at Gurney's Inn, – 'where the sound meets the ocean' - not far from The Montauk Yacht Club. The first night of their long weekend, they dined at the Inn, but already slightly bored, Jordan made reservations at the Yacht Club for the following night.

"We can sit out on the deck with the fire-pits glowing and take in the sunset. How about that, sweetie?"

"Lovely idea, my dahling," Janice replied in her best Peter Sellers 'Pink Panther' voice.

Jordan was used to her sarcasm. It was part of their dynamism.

On that particular Friday, they had a couple of martinis (each) – very dry – on the deck of The Montauk Yacht Club. They were feeling no pain as they approached the *Maitre' d, sommelier,* Alistair Williams at the dining room desk.

Alistair blanched when he saw Jordan Mather and his wife. He could tell there was an air of antipathy between them. (Martinis made with gin could do that!)

Alistair had seen the Mathers before. One blazing hot Friday in the late afternoon in July of '83, when Alistair/Sasha was still Assistant

Manager at the King Kullen supermarket in Eastport, a ruckus occurred, of which Janice Mather was the center.

People, pouring out of a sweltering city seeking beach relief for the weekend, would stop at King Kullen to purchase steaks for the grill, salads, fresh fish to *sauté*, newly baked cakes and rolls. Every Friday in the summer months, the place was a mob scene – and people were rude!

Sasha, from his vantage point behind the glass money office window, could observe the chaotic scene. On that typical Friday late afternoon, he noticed the blonde Janice Mather, standing, about fifth in line, waiting to check out, with a cart loaded and overflowing.

It was slow going, the store a crush of people, when Janice Mather's impatience and frustration took over. She raised her voice and started to yell. "You locals. Why do you come here on a Friday when we come down from the city – tired and hot – and ready to have guests – Why don't you shop during the week – You're Goddamn lucky to have us, bringing a touch of class to your community, this stupid, little village…"

The trouble was, she just wouldn't stop, even though her husband, Jordan Mather was pulling at her arm.

From a customer, farther back in line, a loaf of Wonder Bread flew through the air, aimed at Janice Mather. This was followed by a package of hot dog rolls, from another cart. Soon, there were rolls of toilet paper and Scott Towels, all soft stuff, tossed at the shrieking woman, Janice Mather, who was near hysterics.

Sasha had pressed a button under his desk that alerted the police station, but before any cop appeared, Jordan Mather had managed to support his wife out of King Kullen, leaving the cart with its goods behind. He, apparently, got her into their car, and then returned to the store and went to Sasha's office window and apologized, offering to pay for any damage.

"No problem," Sasha had responded.

He came from behind the window, in his shirtsleeves, as Jordan said, "She just gets upset at all these pushy locals."

"I know where she's coming from," Sasha said with a smile. "Some people just don't know how to behave." He realized too late he could have been speaking of Jordan Mather's wife. So he quickly added, "it's easy to be pushed over the edge," and the two men had shaken hands.

But that was then, a good two years ago. Now? Would Jordan Mather recognize him? The thought made his blood run cold.

In his natty white trousers and blazer, with his clipped moustache, Alistair decided quickly to affect a British accent. He had always been good at imitations, and with a "How di do, Sir and Madame, please come this way," he led the pair, with his back to them, to a table with a view of Lake Montauk. He handed two menus to Janice Mather, who had seated herself, and tried to leave as fast as he could, but not before Jordan gave him a swift, hard glance. "Hey," he said, but Alistair was already headed back to his station at the entrance.

As he seated himself, Jordan exclaimed to Janice, "That guy sure looks familiar."

"What guy?" his wife responded, busy with inspecting the list of dinner specials.

"The *Maitre' d.*"

"Maybe you saw him in another restaurant."

"Uh uh," Jordan mumbled. "No. Somewhere else."

"Oh, come on, Jordan. Maybe the gin got to you. Now the blackened Mahi Mahi looks interesting – and lets get some wine."

"No. I want another martini."

"Okay," she said. "Me too."

And there went the evening…much to Alistair's relief, as he saw the pair teeter out about 9:30, unaware of anything that was around them, least of all, him.

Chapter Nine

SHAKEN NOT STIRRED

Alistair/Sasha was truly shaken by the encounter with the Mathers. They had not fingered him, but he realized, it was a possibility, that other folks from the western towns of the East End might be stopping at The Montauk Yacht Club who could recognize him.

He decided to dye his hair gray. If Scarlet/Jillian could do it, so could he. He even added streaks to his moustache. He practiced his English accent and could speak now as a proper chap from London – "moved to Teaneck New Jersey for family reasons," he would explain if anyone asked. He managed to put on a rather distinguished, older demeanor.

Scarlet was not impressed. "Who do you think you're kidding?" she'd say with a laugh, as he emerged from the bathroom, drying his newly-grayed locks.

"You'd be surprised," he answered with a scowl. "I can fool many an old acquaintance, kiddo!"

"Yeah, maybe, if they didn't know you very well," she responded.

Alistair had told Scarlet of the Mathers' encounter, how he had managed to deceive them. He recounted, with a kind of venom, that it was she, Jillian/Scarlet who was the very one who had crashed the Mather boy, Rodney's, new silver Corvette that had been stolen. It was all her fault.

"It was the ice. I told you. I skidded," she whined.

"Whatever," he replied, "but it's why there was no delivery on it, and

32

why we came under police investigation. It was all your fault, my friend. Your fault."

"Right! You had nothing to do with the whole boondoggle! You were up to your ears in it, Sasha – and you pocketed a whole lot of hundred dollar bills as a result of your dirty deeds."

"Shut up," he shouted at her.

"It's a wonder I still sleep with you," she shouted back. "Not often do you get it up, but who's there for you when you do. Little old me!"

"Aren't you gonna be late for work?" he growled.

"Yeah, and I need a ride."

Alistair/Sasha, combed his damp hair flat, put on his blazer, took out the car keys and opened the door. Scarlet/Jillian followed in miniskirt and red boots. The two drove in silence to Joe's Warm-Up where she got out slamming the door behind her and without a glance back, entered the bar.

It was a little before 5:00 on this summer Saturday evening. There were a number of couples already at the small tables inside the room that smelled of old beer and smoke from cigarettes. It was not an unpleasant smell, if you are into the world of barrooms on summer weekends. Somehow, it reeked of parties that lasted well into the early hours. Although a stale smell, it evoked memories of younger days, youthful nights long past.

Scarlet went behind the bar. She looked at the book of last-night's receipts. 'Not bad,' she thought. Old Joe does quite a business – particularly in this little town.' But then, he should. His was the only real bar in the whole hamlet.

Joe came out from the back office.

"Hey, Scarlet. I like the boots."

"Is that all you like?" she said from under lowered lashes.

Joe laughed, coming over to her. "Well let me see," he said, peeking down her white blouse. Scarlet turned away with a smile. She knew she had him on her string, a string she planned to pull in slowly. This banter had been going on since she first started her job some weeks earlier.

"You expecting a crowd tonight?" she said, all business.

"Yep. Should be. It's summer. It's a Saturday night in July. Better plan to stay late."

"Extra hours!" she said, turning to him.

"Don't worry. I'll keep track. You'll get paid. And by the way, I'll drive you home."

'Uh uh', she thought. 'The usual wrestling match coming!'

Scarlet had told him she was married. (She was not.) She and Alistair were a sham for public consumption. Her 'husband' usually drove her to work, but did not always pick her up. It depended on the hour. If it was late, she would call Alistair at the front desk in the dining room at the Montauk Yacht Club and let him know that Joe would drop her off at the cabin after work.

There was always a tussle in the car if Joe was driver. She let him get away with bits and pieces, but would always claim marriage as a no-no to any further play.

"You're driving me crazy," he would pant. "What can I do to let me at it?"

"Nothing, baby Joe Warm-Up," she would purr, and arriving at the cabin, leave him quickly after a final blistering kiss.

Not this night. After the bar cleared and the lights were turned off, she got in Joe's car and he drove her around the corner – just a few blocks - to his apartment. "I want to show you something," he told her.

"I can guess what," she said with a giggle.

He looked at her. "I wish…but no. I was wondering if you wanted to make a little extra money."

Scarlet sat up at full attention. "You bet!"

They entered Joe's pedestrian one-bedroom home. It was filled with man-clutter – a folded newspaper, a beer can on the floor, shoes next to the lumpy couch.

"It's not much but it works for me. Sorry, it's a mess since the wife left," he mumbled, tossing the empty Bud Lite into a trash basket. "Here, sit down." He gestured toward the couch. "I want to get something."

Scarlet sank down on the much-used piece of furniture. She had no idea what to expect, but Joe quickly returned. He sat down beside her. He was holding something in his right hand.

Looking at her directly, Joe said," You know, Scarlet, I like you. So
do the customers. You have a great way of talking their language and
teasing them – and that's important…particularly in terms of the job I
am going to ask you to do."

"Job?"

"Yeah," and he got to his feet. "Not exactly a job." Joe was standing
in the middle of the floor. "Look. I trust you. This is just between you
and me."

"Hey, you're confusing me. What is it you're proposing?"

He sat down again close to her and opened his right hand. In it, was
a plastic bag enclosing a white, powdery substance. "This."

"Is that what I think it is?"

"Just what do you think it is?"

"White sugar?"

"You can call it that."

"Ah, no. Hey, Joe, I don't think so."

"All I ask is that when one of the customers is looking to score…"

"Girls?"

"No. This!"

"That?"

"This! Smack."

Scarlet got to her feet. She began to pace, the heels of her red boots
clicking on the bare floor. This went on some minutes.

"Will you stop that," Joe demanded, annoyed.

She paused. "You're asking me to push drugs? Heroin? You've got to
be kidding."

"Why not? You're just filling a need. Someone else could do it. I could
do it and I do."

"How do you get the stuff?"

"Hey, Scarlet. This is a fishing village. Some of the boats coming in
have a different kind of haul and it doesn't smell fishy."

"I'll just bet!"

"Certain of our local fisherman go out and meet boats that have
sailed all the way from Cuba or even down from Canada. An exchange
is made."

"For dollars."

"Of course. Look, I'll pay you $50 a pop for any packet you palm off on a customer".

"$50!" she snorted.

"Okay. $100."

"Do the customers know you have this...service?"

"Some do. And then some get the message – you know – kind of whispered around the bar –and suddenly they want it too. You know, Scarlet, it's not just the party-goers – the summer people – it's the regulars too...the locals."

Joe could see that Scarlet was intrigued. Her lips were pursed. She had resumed pacing and the click of heels resumed. He watched the movement of her hips. He licked his lips, suddenly hungry for her, but decided this was not the moment...but those long legs!

"What about the cops?"

Joe laughed. "Well, some of them have a taste for the White Sugar too."

Scarlet stopped and just stood there, regarding Joe. It lasted a long minute. "Let me think about it," she said finally as he watched her. "Hey, I gotta get home."

As they went to the door to leave, Joe said to her, over his shoulder, "By the way, that husband of yours...at the Yacht Club...he might find a user or two, don't you think? Some of those big-rich – they like to play too, no?"

Scarlet did not respond. She was silent all the way home. There was no tussle in the car this night, although Joe reached for her.

Her excuse? "Stop it. Not now, Joe Warm-Up. I'm thinking."

Chapter Ten

SUMMER OF WORK-
SUMMER OF DISMAY

As the busy summer of 1985 progressed, into fall, Violet found her workload at Brandeis Realty not only heavier, but in many ways, extremely rewarding. Because Bethany was so often in Montauk at the new office on The Circle, Violet found herself presiding over closings by herself, and delegating to the other agents, assignments for Open Houses, listing agreements, and the showing of properties. It was heady, this new sense of responsibility, and Violet relished it.

It was a good time for the Roses. The little girl was blooming. Bud was moving in his Deputy Sheriff's automobile from one end of Suffolk County to the other, always with interesting stories to tell his young wife as they sat on their back deck in the evening over a glass of wine.

Violet still called the baby Starfish, in her private moments, as she laid her in her crib. "My little golden star…fish," and she would laugh as she kissed the top of the fuzzy hair on the baby's head, and the little one would burble in response. "You almost sound like lapping water," Violet would murmur back, and the child would burble again, then close her eyes in sleep.

Yes, it was a good time…until a storm of a different kind grew in the distance, slowly, emerging across the East End like a plague, as big as a Nor'Easter and just as dangerous.

Actually, it was happening all over the country, but on Long Island, it had a grip that was growing, affecting the young people, destroying lives, an explosion of misery that became palpable.

It was the scourge of drugs.

The problem was worst in the summer. Those, coming down from New York City, those with the large beach houses, those with communal rentals, all were ready for release from pressure, eager for fun in the sun, and high, happy festivities at night.

Often White Sugar was the focus of the party!

Of course, there were the family types where this did not apply, but, increasingly, as the summer spent itself, the use of recreational opiates had grown in number and intensity.

Bud Rose had a major job to do.

In late June, he had had to break up a loud, angry group in a rented, communal house in Westhampton Beach. The house was set on the bay, opposite Dune Road, and seven young people from the city had taken it to share throughout the summer.

Bud had arrived there, after receiving a call from the Riverhead office. More than one neighbor had called 911 about the noise and ruckus that was going on next door. It was near midnight, and the wind and rain were blowing up quite a storm, churning the bay-waters and matching the turmoil inside the house.

He had found two young men on the floor with bloodied noses. One had lost a front tooth. Two young girls lay drugged out on a couch in the living room, clutching each other, totally out of it.

The other three, a man and two girls, had been sitting there, dazed and drunk. There were liquor bottles on a sideboard, one broken on the floor. An old-fashioned record player was blaring out hideous music (a Metallica recording), and there were signs on the coffee table of white powder, scattered about.

Bud had the sense to taste it. It was just as he thought…heroin.

There was no point in taking them in. He told the least inebriated young man, named Jeremy, that he would be back in the morning to bring them to the station in Riverhead, that Jeremy must see that they were all prepared to go, that if any should try to leave, they would be in much more serious trouble. He took the driver's licenses of all seven and the keys to their two vehicles and left them to sleep it off.

Bud had left disturbed. This was not the first such case – although this was the most serious. And it was still early in the summer. God knows what could be coming next!

It happened soon. It was in early July that a young woman was found dead on the beach near The Swordfish Club. She was determined to be about 17 years old – with no ID – half naked, half in and out of the water. There was a large quantity of drugs in her system. She had OD'd there in the sand.

Soon enough, the parents – name of Barnard – called and reported their daughter missing. They were local residents, the father, a teacher at the Westhampton Beach High School, and the mother, a nurse at the hospital in Riverhead.

Devastated by their loss, they could only give small bits of information through their tears. "She lived at home...she was going to a party..."

"With whom?"

"A new boy she had just met...a boy from New York, just here for summer weekends..."

"Does he have a name?"

"'I think she said Ben...Ben something...I think he had family over in Quogue."

Bud went immediately to see Jordan Mather.

He found him in his garage that abutted the large house on the bay side of Dune Road, opposite the Quogue Beach Club.

"I'm looking for a tool to ream out the fireplace," he said, without even greeting Bud.

"Maybe that garden spade over there, next to the Toyota?" Bud volunteered.

"Yeah. That might do it." Jordan Mather turned to the policeman. "How can I help you?" he said with a smile. "I must say, you did a fine job on the car theft case."

"Thanks. I appreciate that. But I'm here about a rather tragic event that transpired last night. A young girl – a local – name of Susie Barnard – was found dead on the beach near The Swordfish."

"Good God!" Jordan Mather exploded. "Dead?"

"Unfortunately, she'd taken a load of drugs. That's what killed her. Her parents are beside themselves."

"Where'd she get them? And who...?"

"That's what we're trying to find out. The parents said they thought she had a date with a young man from Quogue...first name Ben."

Jordan Mather sat down on an old armchair in the corner of the garage. He was pale. "We have youngsters here at the house – but, thank God, not one of them is named Ben." He literally wiped his brow.

"I hate to ask, but do you know any of your friends and neighbors here in Quogue who might have a boy named Ben?"

Slowly, surely, Jordan Mather began to nod. "I'm afraid so...oh God. And he's quite a handful..."

It came about that the young man in question was an easy mark, into drugs in a big way, much to his parents' disgust, and all too weak to make any kind of protest.

"When she wouldn't wake up, I guess I just ran scared," Ben mumbled, as he was taken in.

Later, it turned out Ben had no idea who supplied the drugs. "They were just there...at the party... everyone took 'em." He paused. "Then, Susie...she and I went down to the beach..." He burst into tears.

Bud Rose was at a loss. As July continued, and August appeared, the local jail, and that in Riverhead, was filled with a large number of young people, taken in for misdemeanors, indecent exposure, drunkenness, fights, even a slashing.

Every one of them had drugs in their system.

Yes, thought Bud. It's a scourge, a storm of inestimable power and danger.

Good old Westhampton Beach just wasn't the same anymore! Oh, of course in the old days, there was booze, there was music sometimes loud, and a bit of marijuana – weed – smoked in the night. Bud, as a youngster, a young man in Westhampton Beach, Long Island, had lived through all that, only a few years ago.

But this? What was happening now – in 1985? This was different. Deep drugs, deadly drugs were beginning to hit hard, dangerous and lethal.

For Bud, in the purview of his job, it was a new and bitter world.

Where did they come from, these drugs of death?

From New York City? Surely. But from where else?

It was time the Deputy Sheriff found out.

Chapter Eleven

MONTAUK

Scarlet had done her thinking, and with the help of Alistair, made the decision to take Joe Warm-up's offer of the nefarious job of pushing dope. She decided the money –$100 a pop – to be more important than the illegality. She knew she was in trouble with the law already, over the automobile scam, so what difference would a little additional misconduct make.

"Just don't get caught," Alistair cautioned. "Drugs are a big deal – bigger than car theft, I can guarantee."

"So?" she snickered.

"By God, be careful! Your being fingered could somehow lead back to your fake husband – ME – and that is unacceptable!" Alistair said this with such a scowl on his face that Scarlet winced.

"Okay, okay. Don't get your knickers into a snarl. I wasn't born yesterday."

"You can say that again," he responded, eyeing her up and down. "But leave me out of it." With that, Alistair Williams started off to work at the Montauk Yacht Club, in his Chevy, dropping Scarlet Williams at the bar off Main Street.

It was now the month of August, 1985, and summer was in full swing. The town was jumping with tourists from every possible category: hippies on motorcycles; folks in trailers; those in SUVs who parked in the State Parks; the rich and famous at Gurney's Inn and at a number of local mansions; honeymooners; motel week-enders; fishing aficionados who chartered boats to test themselves at the sport.

And of course, the locals, who enjoyed a summer party as much as anyone else…if not more.

The smell of barbeque filled the air, along with the sound of live music. Shagwong's Tavern was jammed, with customers bent over their fried calamari and beer, and as for Joe's Warm-Up Bar, it was hard to get a place inside. There was often a line on the street – not a long line, but anxious people, tapping their feet, waiting to get to the stand-up bar at the end of which, a guitar and piano played the latest hits.

Montauk, Long Island on a summer's night!

By now, Scarlet – with Joe Warm-Up's instruction – had devised a system for delivery of 'special' items to particular customers. She wore – over her cut-off jeans or mini-skirt - a white apron, tied around her waist, with two pockets. It had lace trim and was jaunty, even sexy, like a French maid's apron in a burlesque skit.

In one pocket, there were small packets of heroin; in the other pocket, small packets of cocaine. When a customer would beckon her and say, "Hey, Sugar, bring me a bourbon on the rocks (or whatever drink he demanded), she would bring his glass, take a paper cocktail napkin and retrieve from the one pocket a heroin packet with the napkin folded over it, place that on the customers table, putting his glass on top. "Don't want to spill any," she would say with a grin. "Don't want to get anything wet!"

Or another would ask her for "a Coke – and oh, by the way, a gin and tonic to go along with it," with a sly look, and maybe the remark, "make mine a double," and following the same procedure, two cocaine packets in cocktail napkin camouflage would be deposited under the gin and tonic. That was the code.

The bar tabs that followed for these 'consumers,' when presented, were always accompanied by sizeable cash deposits covering the White Sugar and Coke transactions.

On closing the place, Scarlet would meet Joe back in his office and present him with her 'take'.

"Good girl," he would say, with a slap on her bottom. "And here's your share." Sometimes she would take home as much as $900.

It was all working remarkably well for several weeks. Scarlet was bringing home many $100 dollar bills, so many in fact, Alistair was growing jealous.

"'Course it's summer. Probably change after the season," she mused.

"Maybe not," was his reply. "I gather there are a number of locals who enjoy the game."

Scarlet laughed. "You bet…even a couple of cops. Big users."

After Labor Day, and through the early fall, Scarlet's 'take' diminished, but it did not cease. It was still large enough to make her proud and comfortable enough to buy some sweet necessities – lipgloss and silk panty hose and more high-heeled boots in bright patent leather. She loved her new persona.

And so did Joe Warm-Up. In fact, their relationship had heightened to the point of exchanging, not just $100 dollar bills, but personal, physical intimacies, in the back office of the bar. It was becoming a habit that Scarlet really enjoyed, adding a special *frisson* to the whole business of supplying illegal drugs – this sexual *sub-rosa liaison* at Joe's Warm-Up Bar.

Scarlet found her new life delicious, at least, for the moment.

Chapter Twelve

WHITE SUGAR

Heroin. Cocaine

Bud, in the RPD office, was determined to pursue the circuit bringing drugs - on such a high level – to the East End community. It was appalling the number of cases that had come to his attention in just the last few months.

In incarcerating the young people picked up in misdemeanor cases, where drugs always seemed to be an instigator and cause, there had been no breakthrough of exactly how the drugs were acquired.

The suppliers! How many? And who the hell were they?

When a youngster was asked, the usual response was, "It was just there...available...laid out on the table...White Sugar was just part of the party." In other words, none of them seemed to know anything!

As for older offenders, they were fewer and far between. More clever in deception, many denied knowledge of any such 'carrying-on', and unless they agreed to a blood test for drugs, well, there was little a policeman could do. "An invasion of privacy..." said with outrage... and "Do I need a lawyer?"

In fact, only two such subjects – one man in his 50s and an inebriated 30 year-old woman – took the test and were found to have a great deal of alcohol in their systems but little Coke. They were let go. For Bud, this was disheartening.

Finally, the first hint of a breakthrough gave him hope for a way to proceed.

In late August, 1985, there was a 50th birthday party thrown for a man named Milton Kramer, by his wife. It was held at their estate in Quogue. And what a bash!

In a tent decorated as a Flemish tavern with tableaux of Milton Kramer's favorite Hieronymus Bosch paintings, it attracted a glamorous and chic crowd from the summer mansions and from New York City.

Oriental rugs were put down over the grass so that the guests would not get their feet wet. There were gold brocade tablecloths with centerpieces of treasure chests with jewels (fake) overflowing. Candles dripped, as an excellent dance band played, and vintage wines, beers, lagers, and champagne were served. (Also, gin, vodka, scotch, whiskey, brandy).

There were a number of policemen protecting the scene and the expensive automobiles on the grass and driveway of the estate. A cop stood at the entrance where the patrons entered in their finery, diamond bracelets flashing. Bud Rose had been on duty at many such parties in the past, but none so lavish. Now, as Deputy Sheriff, he had no need to be there, except for his own personal reason: White Sugar.

Bud was dressed in a plain suit. He was permitted entrance by the policeman at the front of the canvas tent, which was draped with colorful tapestries (Milton Kramer loved the medieval culture of Flanders – Belgium, the Netherlands -) a fact that dictated the *décor* of the interior festivities.

Bud had decided to just mingle. There were few people he recognized. However, the Mathers were in attendance, Janice, the older glamor girl in a flowered dress. He waved a hello to Jordan. He saw a number of celebrities – Budd Schulberg, the renowned writer, and his wife, who had a house near Turkey Bridge were present, and there were others who seemed 'famous' but Bud was not sure.

There was much air-kissing, and "dahling," emitted from the spiffy crowd in their designer outfits. "I see you're wearing one of mine," shrieked one lady to another. "Who's that?" Bud asked a young woman standing nearby. "Oh that's Carolina Herrera! The famous designer." This meant absolutely nothing to Bud. Maybe Violet would know.

The music played. The people danced on a raised stage. The drinks flowed. The laughter got more intense and louder, and Bud grew more and more tired. He was waiting for something to happen, he did not know what – a packet passed from one hand to another, a small cluster of people engrossed in what? When, suddenly, he saw just that.

Three men were hunched over something in a corner of the tent near a tapestry of a naked woman. Their laughing together stopped as Bud approached. They stepped away, one from the other, two of them each pocketing something. Nodding to Bud, they moved off in separate directions. Bud thought they looked guilty, but why? Did they know he was law enforcement? And who were these men? Where did they come from?

The young 'Carolina Herrera' woman was still close by. Bud went over to her. "Do you happen to know those guys?" he asked. "You seem to know most of the people here," this said with a smile.

"Oh sure," she smiled back. "They came in from Montauk. The big guy – the fat one, he's got a big stake in Gurney's Inn."

"Thanks," Bud said to her, and turned to leave.

"Hey…Haven't I been of help?" she said coyly. "Where're you goin'?"

"Got business. But thanks again. And have fun," he said, indicating the room with dancers twirling, tapestries blowing in the slight wind, and a red-hot band warming up the evening.

Aha, thought Bud. Montauk! The tip of Long Island.

Where the boats come in.

Chapter Thirteen

ALL THE SHIPS AT SEA

Montauk! Boats! They come and go with impunity; Charter boats, Yachts, Jet-skis, a huge fleet of commercial fishermen. From all over the country and up and down the Eastern seaboard, they can sail in and out at will, unchecked by any formal agency.

What better way to transport an illegal substance!

Bud Rose began to follow his gut instinct. He knew that drugs were being brought down from New York City. That was a given. The implication that the far end of Long Island was giving entry to the plague attacking society was a compelling concept, but such a natural, really obvious all along.

Bud made sure the route in his Deputy Sheriff's car included the town of Montauk and Montauk Point… and often!

It was in the early fall of 1985, after the shindig in Quogue for Milton Kramer, that Bud started a regular trip to the far east end. On one such excursion, right after Labor Day, he stopped at Brandeis Realty on The Circle in midtown Montauk.

As he entered the front door, he passed three young women at desks, busily working the phones. Bethany came out of her office at the rear of the building to greet the officer.

"Come in, Bud. Delighted to see you," she said with a smile, extending her hand. "To what do I owe the pleasure? Or have I done something illegal?"

"Not that I know of," he replied with a grin. "Just a courtesy call. Violet told me of your new branch."

"She's working hard in Westhampton. Doing a great job for the business. She really is a gem, Bud." Bethany ushered him into her office and returned to her desk.

"I think so," he said shyly.

"Come. Have a seat," she said, indicating a chair in front of her. "I'm sure there is something else on your mind. Is there any way I can help?"

Bud laughed as he sat down. "Is it that obvious?" He adjusted himself. "There is something. I don't know if you can be of help, but I have to start somewhere. As you must know, we have a big drug problem…"

"Oh, you know summer people," she interjected. "They come here to party…"

"It's more serious than that, I can assure you…a young woman overdosed on the beach in Westhampton…"

"Oh yes. I heard about that…but surely that was a tragic accident."

Yeah," he said bitterly, "a lethal accident. But there are other real crimes being committed in the haze of drugs, I can assure you – break-ins, thefts, beatings. It's gotten to be an epidemic."

"Good lord. I had no idea."

"The Riverhead jail is full of young people who have gone quite nuts. I fear for them – I fear for our community."

"Well, Montauk doesn't seem to be in the throes of any epidemic," she said with a smile. "But I don't really socialize here – except for lunch with clients sometimes. I go home to Westhampton in the evenings usually. I really don't know what happens at night…"

"I can understand that," he said rising. "It's just that – you're a savvy woman – if you should hear or see something suspicious, do let me know. You know, Montauk, with its accessibility to boats from all over this coast, could easily be a place of entry for illegal drugs."

Bethany blanched. "I hadn't thought of that," she said. "Look, I will surely keep my eyes and ears open. You will be the first to know, Bud."

"Here's my number," he said handing her a piece of paper. "By the way, there's a guy who supposedly has a piece of Gurney's Inn that is mighty suspicious."

"Of peddling drugs?"

"Maybe. Don't know his name – but he's about 50 years old and heavy-set. If you hear…"

"That's not much to go on."

"I know," Bud said. "There'll be more information soon, I promise."

Bethany was thoughtful. "What you said… about Montauk being so open to seafaring vessels…it sure does give one pause. I promise to be on the alert." With that, she rose, and led him to the door of her office.

Bud left The Circle and drove his car over to Gurney's Inn.

It was not far, The Inn on Old Montauk Highway, about a mile or two from Hither Hills State Park in one direction, and downtown Montauk in the other.

Bud parked in the lot next to the driveway and entered the building. The entrance was large, elegant, but he noticed, with a 'used' look, as if the sofas and chairs had suffered much activity and were in need of refurbishing. He walked to the front desk and spoke to the young woman in attendance, asking her if the manager was available.

"Who wants to know?" was the curt reply.

Bud, in slacks, t-shirt, and leather jacket, produced his Sheriff's badge, and the girl, flustered, said, "Oh, sorry, Sir. The manager -Martin Eldridge - will be back around 2:OO. Would you care to go in and get some lunch until then?"

"I think I will," Bud said. "Please tell Mr. Eldridge I want to see him," and with that, he headed toward the ocean by way of a ramp-like walkway, which led to an outer deck with umbrella-capped tables.

Seated under his bright covering, watching the magnificent blue water lapping at the sand, Bud was reflective. Down on the beach, he saw a young woman in a bikini lying on a palette with a male masseur from The Inn rubbing her skin with oil. A fast motorboat was causing white caps farther out on the ocean. A long wooden dock extended into the water farther down on the left. What a perfect world!

Were drugs here at this salubrious place, around the corner, available to the girl on the beach, the boy in the motorboat? How could the scourge that hit and bit at the people of this earth, young and old, be allowed to continue, causing such destruction of lives. Bud shook his head.

Looking at the bright wavelets, he was reminded of how the sea– so gentle at this moment –so serene - was deceptive. It could rise in violence and destroy all before it. Bud had seen its fury – more than once.

A young man approached with long white apron tied about his waist. "Lunch, sir?" was the cheery question he asked, proffering a menu.

"Why yes," Bud said, glancing at the list before him. "I'll have the lobster roll – and an iced tea."

"Excellent choice," and the waiter went off to his task.

Bud sat there. He was contemplating the interview with Mr. Eldridge, fully aware that, often, in these luxurious enclaves the manager, the *Maître d'*, even the valet parker, could be a purveyor of illicit pleasures for the clientele – at a price, of course.

When his lobster roll appeared, loaded with the succulent meat, the bits of celery, the lemony mayonnaise on a toasted roll, he forgot for a moment his dilemma.

Soon enough, his thoughts returned to Mr. Eldridge. Bud did not want to give away too much information regarding the drug distribution, but he did want to get a sense of what or what not the manager knew.

Mr. Eldridge, a slim man in his mid-40s, suddenly came out of the walkway and onto the deck and saw Bud Rose at his table. He came forward and introduced himself.

"Do sit down," Bud said.

"Unless you wish to go to my office," Mr. Eldridge said.

"No, no, not necessary – and it's so pleasant here in the sun."

"I see you're enjoying one of our specialties."

"And indeed it is special. Absolutely delicious. I'm eating every crumb." Bud wiped his mouth. "I'm here because I wanted to find out from you – as manager – if you have become aware, recently, of any displays of unusual behavior in your clients."

"I don't understand," Mr. Eldridge said. "Most of our people are well-to-do – this is a pretty expensive resort – lots of amenities – the spa – the pools – and of course the gorgeous beach. There isn't a lot of drama – if that's what you mean. Certainly no murders," he said with a kind of silly laugh.

"Of course not," Bud laughed along with him. "But there must be the occasional excessively rowdy exchange, or a drunken fight or two…"

"Well, yes, that does happen in the course of a late night summer party, but nothing…extreme."

Bud realized that Mr. Eldridge looked suddenly quite uncomfortable.

"Is it from booze, do you think?"

"Yes, yes, booze," Mr. Eldridge said, nodding his head vigorously. "Sometimes the rich do over-indulge."

"Well, I guess we all do from time to time," Bud said, as Mr. Eldridge got to his feet.

"I hope I've been of some help."

"Oh, you have. Here let me give you my phone number. If anything untoward should happen…you know…like a drug shipment coming in on one of those fishing boats…or even on a yacht… you would let me know, now wouldn't you?"

"A drug shipment!" Mr. Eldridge exclaimed, turning quite red. "Drugs? Why…I can't believe that sort of thing could happen! Naturally, I would let the police know. But it's highly unlikely, highly," he gasped, turning on his heel and leaving the deck.

Bud finished his iced tea.

'Hm', he thought. 'That good Mr. Eldridge got mighty nervous there. Methinks he doth protest too much. Something about him just doesn't smell right'. And he called the waiter over for the tab.

Chapter Fourteen

OH, LITTLE DAUGHTER

For some reason, all that Bud Rose could think of, on his drive back to Westhampton, was Starfish. He called her that now. Her name was no longer Aurora or Rori to him. Starfish was part of the sea to which he knew he and Violet belonged. Everything Bud did and felt related to this small, sea urchin of a daughter who had captured his heart.

The thought of Jillian Burns, the biological mother, haunted him, her death perhaps a blessing in disguise. However, the possibility that Jillian's genes, her persona, could be ingrained in his child, hurt him. Violet, with all her loving motherly ways assuaged much of his fears, but not all.

The thought of his baby's future motivated Bud Rose in ways he would never have surmised. The idea of a homeland cursed with drugs – that young girl OD'd on the beach – the kids in the jail in Riverhead – was this to be her destiny? He shivered as he drove.

The faster he went, the more determined he grew to crack the hideous scourge that permeated the whole of Long Island. In his mind, he went over his discoveries of the day. Bethany Brandeis might well be a conduit of information. She was so aware of those around her and of their hidden motives, that Bud was sure he had a wire in the field. She was a smart woman.

As for that Eldridge fellow, he surely displayed a kind of guilt. Oh, it was nothing he said. It was in his nervous demeanor, particularly when Bud had mentioned the ocean ships as possible purveyors of drugs.

There was that long wharf right down the beach so close to Gurney's Inn, an easy landing spot for every type of boat - and under the cover of darkness?

Bud decided his imagination was running away with him, but he also determined, that on his next trip, he would approach the fishing-boat wharves that lined the lower section of the town of Montauk. Located on the water, a long raised walkway was where the fishermen docked with their catch, each with a separate mooring. There were also boats for charter available at small piers, all in a row, a variety of seaworthy transport for the eager tourist, and each at a different cost.

It was all very concentrated and convenient.

This set up reminded him of Greenport, the town on the North Fork on the way to Orient Point. The wharf arrangement was so similar, and again, the fishing fleet and party boats came into that village almost as frequently as into Montauk.

What a load of ground to cover! He decided to assign two other Deputy Sheriffs to this assignment. It was impossible to do it alone. He recognized that fact, but it only whetted his determination.

"I have to protect her, Starfish, my daughter," Bud muttered aloud, and he shivered again.

Violet's father, George Annas, was another one who called her by that name. Starfish. George has lost his renegade son, Sasha, to the sea in that terrible accident during the storm, ROSE, or so he believed. George Annas had felt bereft for months.

Later, to see his little granddaughter, paddling in the shallow water lapping the beach in the cove of Moriches Bay near Bud and Violet's house in Remsenburg, well, it touched his heart.

'She's born for the water. She's born of the sea,' George said to himself, as he watched his daughter, Violet, splashing water over the child's tummy, as she gurgled, golden in the sand. 'Little Starfish.'

Bud Rose arrived home just before dark. Violet and his child were there to greet him. He held them tight, more precious to him than ever he thought possible.

"She played in the water today – in the cove. How she loved it," Violet said.

"I would expect no less," Bud said, his heart tightening.

"There were two starfish on the sand. She was enchanted with them."

However, with all Violet's love and respect for the sea, there was fear, as well, deep in her soul, of the violence beneath those waves. She had seen it rise and overcome all in its path, pulling houses with people inside from shore, crushing buildings, and bringing all to the maw of its depths.

Violet had been only six years old when she first saw that happen, a Nor'easter that hit Westhampton Beach and caused damage and death. In a house that was uprooted and taken out to sea, she had heard the wails of the persons inside and the sound of a child's cry, a sound that stayed with her for her lifetime.

Chapter Fifteen

LUKE

He came into Joe's Warm-up often — at least twice a week - Luke Erickson - a fisherman who had plied the local waters since his youth. He wasn't young anymore, but his grizzled face, with its weather beaten lines, made him look old.

He had frequented the bar over many years— for the booze – for the music – for the conversation with fellow fishermen and tourists in the summer. Now he came for Scarlet.

She recognized the lust in the eye. He would tease her, speaking of her boots, her lacy apron, the little black bow tie at her throat above the cleavage. However, he never touched her, just smiled whenever she approached, and she would smile back.

She brought him his bourbon, and the occasional packet of White Sugar (not often), and he would grin at her and say, "Lookin' fine tonight Scarlet. Just fine." Or, "Love to take you for a ride on my boat…and I do mean a ride," this said lasciviously. But again, he never so much as laid a finger on her, or even brushed her hand when she laid down his drink.

"Might get seasick," she would tease back. "Too bumpy for me out there on those waves."

"Let's pick a calm day…one with no …bumps."

Scarlet would just grin at him, and twirl away, red boots glistening and apron a-swing.

As summer-time weather diminished and fall colored the leaves, business at the Warm-Up Bar and at The Montauk Yacht Club softened but still continued at a slower pace. Joe Warm-up and Scarlet had more time to amuse each other in his back office.

Alistair had no idea of Scarlet's latest temptation, nor would he have really cared. They still shared a connubial bed, but encounters were few and lackluster.

No. Alistair/Sasha only cared about Alistair's persona – more and more British - more and more elegant, with the pepper and salt head of hair, the gray striped moustache.

Alistair had succumbed to Joe Warm-Up's racket. It took him a bit of time to decide, but the money was irresistible. He arranged for Scarlet to bring him small boxes of heroin and cocaine packets. He had several blazers made to order, each with a large inner pocket and two large pockets on the sides, in which he apportioned a number of the White Sugars and Cokes – separately.

He wore his made-to-order jacket at the entrance of the dining room. As *Maitre d'*, a position he relished, he attempted to appear as elegant as his environs.

One late September evening, the ubiquitous Mr. Reynolds with yet another sexy looking 'daughter', dined at his usual window table. The two stayed late, lingering over a second bottle of Merlot, then brandies. When Mr. Reynolds' young lady made a wobbly retreat to the Lady's Room, the gentleman approached Alistair.

"Ahem. *Maitre d'*. It's Alistair, isn't it?" said with a sly, sidelong grin.

"It is, Mr. Reynolds. Can I be of help?"

"Well, I don't know. That depends." Mr. Reynolds took out his wallet and was opening it. "You wouldn't have something to make a party special? You know...and..." He grinned maniacally.

"Viagra?" Alistair almost whispered.

"No. No!" was the vehement response. "Don't need that... Take a look at my companion!" he said with a leer. " I mean White Sugar?"

"Oh, oh," said Alistair, laughing, reaching into his left-hand pocket and passing the smack to Mr. Reynolds. "That's easy," Alistair continued, "but don't tell anyone," a conscious remark that he knew was the best way to have Mr. R. noise it around to his friends.

"Thanks a bunch," the man said, passing a wad of cash to the *Maitre d'*.

How Alistair wished he'd started this game earlier in the summer, when the place was a hot spot for summer games, but he was happy now. The winter would be lucrative. The regulars – like Reynolds - still came to The Montauk Yacht Club in colder weather, and they all seemed eager to play.

Chapter Sixteen

GUS BRANDT

Gus Brandt had been the lawyer for several of Bethany Brandeis Real Estate closings. Since her opening of the branch in June, the realtor had found, listed, and sold a number of expensive properties in the Montauk area. Business was booming.

Always, after the final meeting of buyer and realtor and lawyer, where Bethany handed over the keys to the house, and money was committed and the deal was done, Gus and Bethany would repair to Shagwong's Tavern for the soft shell crab sandwich for her and fried calamari for him and a quantity of red wine for them both. They would toast their good fortune, flirt outrageously, and have a celebratory time together, he wanting more from her, she playing coy.

In late September 1985, a grand house was purchased (through Brandeis Realty) near Culloden Point, a small peninsula north of Montauk, on the east side of Fort Bay Pond. The buyer, a rather obese man named John Grunwald was a New York City Real Estate Magnate. "I build buildings – tall buildings – the tallest buildings" was his boast. He also had a suite at Gurney's Inn. "I like it out here," he had told Bethany, "but now I want something permanent."

Bethany Brandeis and her lawyer for her realty firm, Gus Brandt, were fair game to the tycoon. As usual, he bested them "Got the house for a song!" John Grunwald chortled to himself with great satisfaction. He especially liked the anonymity the building afforded him, hidden away among trees, lost to prying eyes.

The house was a beautiful four-bedroom, modern, with enormous glass windows overlooking the beach, with private access, and the bay below. It also was set deep, among large trees and bushes, unusual for the local terrain. Bethany was in a rare mood, as expansive in demeanor as was the house! And Gus Brandt received her lavish mood with great good humor and pleasant surprise.

Gus decided to make his move, and Bethany decided to let him.

Bud Rose's visit and his discussion of the drug problem had given Bethany pause. She figured that of all people, Gus Brandt, who had lived in Montauk the better part of his adult life, would surely know of, or at least have a sense of what was going on in the narcotics world of Montauk hamlet. She had to figure a discreet way to approach the subject with him, and one of her all-time weapons for just this sort of thing was intimacy.

As the two sat at the table over lunch, as the time passed and their heads were nearly touching, and their hands were not far apart, Gus posed the question to Bethany, "Why don't you stay over tonight? We could go to The Montauk Yacht Club for dinner. It's quite special."

"I've not been there," she said. "But I don't know, Gus. I hate driving back to Westhampton so late."

"You don't have to, sweetheart. Stay with me." He took her hand in his. "Ya know it's about time."

"About time for what?" she asked, with a dazzling smile as if she knew exactly his meaning.

"Aw, what a tease," he said, grinning, leaning over to kiss her parted lips.

That did it. She stayed. In fact they did not go out to dinner at all. They went directly to his apartment on the south side of Montauk Highway. It was small, stylish, very masculine, but the bed was enormous and fluffy.

It was later, in the kitchen, as she scrambled eggs in a pan and seared some bacon in another, that she brought up the subject of drugs. Bethany knew that Gus was quite delirious with her at the moment, and she determined that now was the time to speak.

As she ladled out the midnight breakfast, she said, "Gus, I have a serious question for you."

"Lay it on me, baby," he said. "Anything you want." He started in on the eggs.

"I had a visit from a Sheriff recently."

"You in trouble?" He looked up, concerned.

"No, no, nothing like that. In fact, he's a friend. His wife happens to work for me in my Westhampton Beach office. No. It's that he got me really worried. You know, a girl OD'd from heroin on the beach there, earlier this summer. A young girl! It was tragic, and Bud, that's the officer's name, he and the whole Riverhead Sheriff's Department are working on the problem of drugs in our community."

"Wow. That's heavy! God, this was good. I've eaten it all. Hey, you can cook too!" Gus exclaimed, smiling at her.

"I'm serious, Gus."

"Yeah. I can tell."

"Is there much going on here in Montauk?"

He was silent.

"Do you know anything? Anyone?

"Well, honestly, there probably is stuff going on. You know, people come down here to relax, have a good time. Can't altogether blame them, now can you?"

"That's not the point. It's a big problem, according to Bud. Lots of young people getting hooked."

"I don't know what you want me to do about it, Bethany."

"At least you could take it seriously."

"I'll try," he said sardonically. "All I know is that I don't do drugs. I do know there are people down here who can get them for you…if you're so inclined."

"Where do those people – those pushers…"

"Ah, come on. They're not 'pushers'…suppliers, maybe. They're providing a service…"

"Well, who are they?"

"You gonna rat me out to your Sheriff friend?"

"Oh course not."

"Then why do you need to know?"

She did not respond at first, then, "Where do they get the stuff? From New York City?"

"Some, I guess. But you forget our boating trade. Montauk has the largest commercial and recreational fishing fleets in New York State. Boats come in from…everywhere…Cuba maybe…Canada…maybe?"

"How do you stop it?"

"You can't, sweetheart. You can't!" He stood up from the table where he had been sitting eating his eggs and bacon. Gus went over and took her in his arms. "Hey, enough of this. Why don't you stay another couple of days. We can go to the Yacht Club for dinner. It's really elegant – great French food – and the bar out on the deck – well it's super to look at the moon…How about it?"

He kissed her. "And a little more of this?" he said, touching her where he had touched her before and where she couldn't resist.

Chapter Seventeen

ALISTAIR'S DOUBLETAKE

He had seen Bethany Brandeis around the town of Westhampton Beach in that other life. He had seen her at the wedding of Violet and Bud Rose, when he played Best Man. Bethany was wearing a red dress, he remembered, but he had never spoken to her.

The sight of her now, approaching the entrance to The Montauk Yacht Club dining room, made Alistair freeze in place. Bethany Brandeis. My God. My sister Violet's boss! What the hell is she doing here?

The consternation flowing through Alistair's head as she neared his station, with lawyer Gus Brandt beside her, left the *Maitre d'* speechless. Would she recognize him? Would she blow the whole facade he had created for himself? Underneath the dandy jacket he was wearing, he was sweating.

Because Bethany had sipped more than one Tequila Sunrise on the outer deck of the Club, watching a starlit night with her new lover, she was quite oblivious to the middle-aged (gray haired) Englishman who showed them a table in the dining room. Sasha Annas never crossed her mind. Her thoughts were on the potential of lovemaking to come, after a superior dinner.

Alistair realized he had passed the test.

He stopped sweating.

Gus and Bethany were deep in conversation over their shrimp *Scampi* and lamb chops. It was a long dinner, finishing with *Tiramisu* and snifters of brandy. As they rose to leave, she asked Gus to make a reservation with the *Maitre d'* for the next night. She had found the *ambiance* and the exquisite food delicious at The Montauk Yacht Club.

After the second brandy, she had promised Gus she would stay another day or two just to be with the lawyer, in his comfortable little apartment and luscious bed.

"You'll stay? Really?" Gus was thrilled. "And we'll eat here again! Now, let me get you home, baby, and now!"

Bethany was delighted with his eagerness. It matched her own.

As they left, Gus spoke quietly to Alistair, reserving the same corner table for the next evening... "around 7:30."

He passed him a $20 bill. "Hey, where you from in England?"

"Liverpool," Alistair mumbled, bowing his head.

"Hmm. Been to London...but never Liverpool. Anyway, see you *manana*." Alistair heard Gus say to Bethany, "Hey, the guy's from Liverpool. Ever been to England? Maybe we should go," and the couple passed out of hearing range.

Whew!

The rest of the evening for Gus and Bethany did not disappoint. In fact it was quite transporting for both of them, and the glow reached over into the next day, which included a sightseeing boat ride around the harbor, past the fishermen's wharves, where some of her euphoria was stemmed when she found the piers dirty with smelly fish parts and loaded with heavy equipment and nets.

"Wow. Suddenly the business of fishing is all too real!" she exclaimed.

"You can say that again. It's tough work, but the men who do it are impassioned. Don't know why, but somehow, the sea is their home."

After a wine-infused lunch at Shagwong's which Bethany now considered 'their place', the two repaired to Gus's apartment. There were many small slaps and tickles along the way and a generous nap in the afternoon.

Real Estate was far from Bethany's mind, right along with the 'drug infestation' that Bud Rose had spoken about. As evening approached, however, and as she returned to earth, at least somewhat, she decided to re-introduce the question of drugs to Gus once again. The thought of the young dead girl on the Westhampton beach stayed in her consciousness in an unexpected way.

Besides, Bethany was a curious woman. She had always had 'a need to know', and just who was involved in poisoning her Long Island world was suddenly vitally important to her.

As she brushed her hair and made up her rosy, flushed face, she determined that over dinner, she would force out of Gus information regarding the Montauk drug trade.

It was off to The Montauk Yacht Club once more. Alistair was prepared for the re-entrance of Gus Brandt and Bethany Brandeis, although he realized, as they approached, that she gave him a hard, quizzical glance, and looked about to speak.

"Hi, Mr. Liverpool. Back again as planned," Gus bellowed as they neared.

"Tonight, we'd like to order a bottle of champagne."

"Of course," Alistair responded in his most British tones. Why was she still looking at him, he wondered, and she was.

As they sat at their corner table, with a spectacular view of the water, Bethany was preoccupied. For some reason, the *Maitre d'* seemed vaguely familiar to her.

"How about the lobster in butter sauce tonight, baby? Might be good with the champagne." The gorgeous vintage champagne had arrived in its ice-cold bucket, which Alistair opened and began to fill their glasses. While he performed this ritual, Bethany never took her eyes off his face.

"Have you been up-island?" she asked Alistair softly. His hands were unsteady but he did not spill the wine.

"Not often, Ma'am. Me and the wife…we stay pretty much here in Montauk," and he managed a smile.

"Interesting," she said, as he quickly left to go back to the front desk.

"What's interesting?" Gus said, absorbed in the menu.

"That man."

"What man."

"The *Maitre d'*. I feel like I've seen him somewhere."

"Lobster in butter sauce? It says here, it's out of the shell and straight into a pan with butter... maybe a salad first. Yeah. A Caesar Salad. Sound good to you?"

"Fine, Gus. Fine."

Over the bright, tasty greens and croutons, Bethany brought up the subject of drug proliferation. "Who's doing this, Gus? It's really a horrible problem."

"Even if you're right, what can we do about it? It's a fact of the way we live now."

"It's not a fact I'm just going to accept. Who are these people, Gus?"

He laid down his fork. "Okay. Okay. Promise me you'll stop bugging me if I take you somewhere after dinner to where some of the action takes place, Okay? Deal? Come on, now, let's eat and enjoy this delicious food."

She raised her glass to her companion. "You're a doll, Gus. I knew you were. Cluing me in, that's really special," she said with a smile. With that, she devoured the succulent lobster dish.

They finished the champagne. "Shall we get a brandy?" she asked.

"Not here. We'll have something where I'm taking you. I'm warning you, it's a totally different deal than this Montauk Yacht Club," Gus said with a sweep of his hand. "Yeah," he repeated as he arose, "a totally different deal."

Chapter Eighteen

PREMONITIONS

It was crowded at Joe's Warm-Up Bar, but then it was a Friday night in the fall of 1985, and everyone was still out to have a good time. Bethany and Gus managed to squeeze into a tiny booth just off the entrance. A young man in black tee shirt was their waiter, bringing them each a brandy.

"Hey, fella. Bring over the bottle, would you?" Gus said with a smile.

The waiter did as he was told. He was sullen.

"What a sour-puss," Bethany muttered.

"Well, look. He's got a lot of competition." Gus pointed a finger at the tall, red-haired waitress. "That's Scarlet. She gets the tips. She gets the attention." Then Gus whispered, "and she provides the smack."

"Smack? Where does she get it?"

"Oh, she's not the supplier. That's Joe himself – the owner. But she's the conduit. She must get a good dollar for the service. I'd bet on it."

"Wow!" Bethany was disturbed. She didn't know why. Something was so strange. She watched the way Scarlet moved and walked, the way she grinned, her lipgloss glowing, the short red hair tousled on her head. She was hard to miss in her thigh-high boots and red mini-skirt, white lace apron and black tie around her throat. She twirled between the tables, bending low to put a drink on a table, careful with the napkins, the packets unseen.

Bethany was absorbed in observing this woman named Scarlet. There was something about her that was reminiscent of...just who?

Bethany couldn't put her finger on it, but it was the second time in one evening that she felt haunted by a sense of *déjà vu*.

First, the *Maître d'* at The Montauk Yacht Club. And now, here at Joe's Warm-Up. Two people! Already seen! Somewhere. Somewhere else. Bethany took a big swig of brandy. It did not help her sense of unrest.

In reality, Bethany had only seen Jillian/Scarlet on occasion emerging from the Sheriff's Office across from Brandeis Realty on the Main Street of Westhampton Beach. It was a couple of years ago – and even last year – before the big storm, ROSE, that Bethany had any awareness of a woman called Jillian. It was only after Bethany learned that the husband of her employee, Violet, Bud Rose, had fathered an illegitimate child with Jillian, that she even knew her name.

And she had glanced at Jillian at the Rose's wedding reception at the Patio, but they had never exchanged a word.

At this moment, in Joe's Warm-Up Bar, over another brandy or two, Bethany made no connection, none at all. But she did know certain facts she had to reveal to Deputy Sheriff, Bud Rose. She decided that he had to interrogate Joe of Joe's Warm-Up Bar, and maybe Scarlet too. After all, Gus said, Scarlet was the conduit.

Bethany did not inform Gus Brandt of this decision. After all, she did not want to terminate the sexual haze he provided her. It was just too intoxicating.

"It's amazing," Bethany said. "The contrast between the Montauk elite and the fishermen is as stark as the ocean itself."

"Yeah," Gus responded. "It's a brutal and selfless life. They're so different from the self-serving and spoiled types at the Montauk Yacht Club, and the mansions overlooking the beach."

"You can say that again," she said, looking around at the leathery faces of some of Joe Warm-Up's regulars.

"Fishing as a way of life is tough and wet and long – but the ocean world of fish and waves and sun and sea is a siren call for all who choose it."

"You sound almost romantic, Gus," she said with a little laugh. "Poetic."

"Well," he responded almost shyly. "I respect them."

"Apparently," Bethany answered. She was truly affected by the rough appearing, scraggy looking fellows at Joe Warm-Up's Bar.

Oh, there were some ordinary people in the place too, Montauk hamlet being a place of families, carpenters, small business owners, in proper attire, or in jacket and jeans.

Then, of course, there were the fishermen, who clustered next to the bar itself. They had their own particular code of dress, their trousers and heavy shirts stained with briny water and slop from pails. They smelled of fish. A common joke around town: 'Montauk's a drinking town with a fishing problem.'

One old codger in particular, who was holding forth at the bar, caught her attention.

"Look at that fellow," she said to Gus. "If that isn't a fisherman by trade…"

Yeah," said Gus. "That's Luke. He's been around forever."

The two simultaneously noticed Scarlet move over to the fellow named Luke, her hand on one hip and a coy smile.

"Why she's teasing him," Bethany said, laughing. "Do you see that, Gus? She's flirting with him."

"Yeah, and by the look on his face, he's lapping it up like a hungry dog. Hey, let's polish off the rest of this bottle…and then home…I've got a little lapping up to do myself," this said with Gus's lascivious little smile that Bethany quite liked. It promised pleasure to come.

Before they could leave, the door at the back of the bar – the door to the office – opened, and Joe, the owner appeared. Bethany found him attractive in a rough way – lean, middle 50s, with dark eyes and an intense demeanor.

Joe saw Gus, gave a small wave, and approached the pair.

"Meet Bethany Brandeis," Gus said, and she put out her hand to meet Joe's.

"Well, Gus. I must say your taste is improving. This is some classy lady," Joe said with a smile.

Bethany smiled back. She was not sure how to feel. This – this Joe – he was a drug supplier? That was all she could think of, as he held her hand a little too long, a little too tightly.

"Bethany has the new real estate office, over on The Circle."

"Ah. Hope you'll visit my bar often, Miss Bethany. It's always open to you."

She just nodded. Then, turning to Gus, "I think we'd best be going," and to Joe, "Nice to meet you. This is such an interesting place. I'm sure I'll be back."

"You'd better," was Joe's parting remark.

As Bethany went through the door to the street, the air hit her with a decisive freshness, a sobering jolt. It was almost October, and September was cooling down. It was a relief to be outside the hot and teeming bar. All she could think of, as she and Gus strolled arm and arm back to his apartment, was Joe the pusher. 'Oh yes,' she said to herself. 'It may not be me who returns, but Joe is surely going to have an unexpected visitor with a pair of handcuffs in his pocket'.

With that thought, Bethany went home with Gus, to bed down with him in forgetfulness.

Chapter Nineteen
STORM BREWING

Bud was driving on the Old Montauk Road down to Montauk hamlet on a Monday afternoon. He had received a call from Bethany Brandeis, saying it was important that he see her, that she had some interesting news.

The rain was pouring, and even in the heavy Deputy Sheriff's vehicle, the wind was trying to pull the car off the road. Bud swerved the wheel. 'It's a big one coming in', he thought. 'Another Nor'easter! Let's hope it's not as bad as ROSE, last spring. That was a doozy'.

It was October and bad weather often hit Long Island in the fall, spring too and summer, sometimes. Bud managed to arrive at The Circle office around 3:00 in the afternoon. Bethany Brandeis was waiting for him.

When she greeted him at the door of Brandeis Realty, he noticed she seemed agitated, on edge. She took him into an inner room and sat behind her desk, indicating the chair on the other side. "Do sit down, Bud," she said. "Before you do, shut the door, if you would." He complied.

"I called because I had a very strange evening with my lawyer last week. He and I have become friends." The way she said this, Bud knew she was more than a little involved with the guy.

"He handles any closings and all legal matters for the branch here in Montauk," Bethany explained.

"A strange evening? How strange?"

"Well, Gus – that's his name – took me to a place called Joe's

Warm-Up Bar. It's popular with locals – has been there for years. Gus introduced me to Joe, the owner. Gus told me that he…well, he supplies packets of dope to any customers who want it…has been doing so for some time. I thought you should know. It might be useful…

"Oh, Bethany, it is. You have no idea. This is the first tangible connection."

"There's also a red haired waitress there who Gus says is the conduit. You know, does the actual exchange."

"Interesting."

"It's funny. There was something about her…well familiar. I can't put my finger on it. Just the way she moved."

"Hmm," was Bud's response.

"Also, earlier, we had dinner at The Montauk Yacht Club – very elegant. And the *Maitre d'*, he too reminded me of someone, but I have no idea who. Or maybe I'm just getting spooked by this whole drug business." She laughed.

"No, no," Bud exclaimed. "Instinct is a powerful tool. And I really appreciate your input here. I will be sure to follow up."

"That's about it," Bethany said, rising from her desk chair. "Thanks for coming all this way."

"No, Thank you," said Bud, as she led him to the door. "You've been very helpful. You'll be hearing from me."

"Please! Do let me know what happens with all this. I am truly interested. It's so important to the community."

"Particularly the young," he said. "It's a war."

After a couple of stops in Southampton, on a burglary case, Bud drove back to his home in Remsenburg. The storm had abated somewhat, which made him relax. He mulled over the facts Bethany had presented to him. There was no question he would return as soon as he could. Joe's Warm-up Bar would be his primary destination. It was interesting what she had said about The Montauk Yacht Club, and Gurney's Inn was suspicious as well. There was a lot to attack in Montauk.

Bud turned on the radio to some soft music. He could not help but think of Starfish, the little girl who would grow up, hopefully, in a less drugged-up world. It bothered him so to think of innocence lost – and worse. Bud would do anything in his power to protect this precious little creature...his Starfish.

On his arriving home, he could not wait to embrace his wife and daughter. Their safety and pureness of life were paramount to him.

He suddenly heard Violet's voice. "Bud, you haven't heard a word I said!"

"I'm sorry, sweetheart."

"What happened down there? You seem so preoccupied."

"What were you saying?"

"I was telling you that our little girl walked a few steps, today," Violet said with a laugh. "Well, not exactly walked...more, she tottered."

"Aw," he said. I hate to have missed those first steps."

"Well, there are surely plenty more to come. But I set her down, standing, and moved away and she tottered across to me – only about three steps, and fell into my arms. She was so proud! A big smile...and see, she's getting teeth on the bottom."

Bud turned away. There were tears in his eyes.

Chapter Twenty

SCARLET FEVER

Deputy Sheriff Bud Rose walked into Joe's Warm-Up Bar on a side street off Main in the hamlet of Montauk. It was a Thursday night in October. The place was busy with local imbibers – mostly fishermen – who considered Joe's Warm-up a second home, after, of course, the sea.

It was near 9:00 in the evening. Bud was in uniform, and when he entered, the bar quieted down, from a surly roar to a quiet kind of whisper.

Bud went to the bar and asked the man tending it to please tell the owner, Joe, he would like to speak with him. The young man behind the counter immediately went to Joe's office door at the rear of the bar, opened it, and yelled, "Someone to see you, Joe. It's important."

Through the door, which was half ajar, Bud could see a man, presumably Joe, in a lounger chair, with the back of a woman straddling him as he sat.

She had bright red hair in a shag-cut.

'Hmm,' thought Bud. 'Joe's a busy fellow – I guess he has a number of rackets.'

Bud could see the girl dismount and Joe rise. Adjusting his clothing, Joe walked toward the door, which he exited, closing it behind him.

It was with a curious, apprehensive look that Joe approached the Deputy Sheriff. "What's up?" were his first words. Then, "Can I help?"

"Well, I don't know. Can you?"

Joe smiled. He had a certain charm, a friendliness that exuded from him that attracted his many clients. "Maybe...if I know what we're talking about?" Again, a smile.

"We're talking about White Sugar." Bud noticed Joe's ruddy face paled. "Is there somewhere we can talk in private?"

"Well, my office is occupied for the moment."

"I noticed," Bud said, at which the color came back to Joe's face. He blushed.

"We can step outside. It's not too cold."

"Fine," Bud agreed, and the two men proceeded through the silent barroom, under the level gazes of twenty or more leathery-faced seamen.

Once on the pavement, standing beside the sign with the words JOE'S WARM-UP BAR in bright red, the two paused, Joe awkward in stance, Bud, casual as he leaned against the doorjamb at the entrance.

Finally, the Deputy Sheriff said, "White Sugar."

Joe did not respond. He paced in place, one foot lifting, then the other. Finally, "What about it?"

"I've been informed that you are able to acquire packets of the substance and are supplying it to...customers? Am I mistaken?"

"Informed? By who?" Joe was furious. His first thought was the redheaded lady with whom he had just been *in flagrante*. 'Just what did that bitch say? And to a cop?' were his first thoughts.

"WHO is not the point, Joe. You know, Long Island is in the midst of a huge problem with drugs – particularly among the young people..."

"Well, Joe's Warm-Up doesn't cater particularly to the young. We are here for the local fishermen and their families – for tourists in the summer – the businessmen in our community who need a 5:00 o'clock whiskey."

"Sure, sure, Joe. So you don't get many youngsters, but it isn't only the young. The very people you mention might also have a taste for White Sugar, even Coke, now couldn't they? I mean, they're only human too."

Joe was unresponsive. He finally blurted out, "I guess so."

"You guessed right," said Bud. "So you DO supply." It was a statement, not a question.

Joe looked diminished. He seemed to grow smaller. "I never used myself. Don't like the loss of control."

"That's not what I'm asking." Joe touched him on the shoulder. "Look, I know you're the little guy, trying to make a buck and this is a means to that end. It's not you we're looking to put the screws on. It's the pushers, the guys who bring in the stuff illegally, the creeps who make the real money - in fact, huge money. They are the ones we have to stop."

Joe was silent for a moment. "I read about the dead girl on Westhampton Beach earlier this summer."

"And she's not the only one."

"God."

"Look, Joe. I'll give you immunity if you help me get to the big boys, the ones who are poisoning our well, here on Long Island, the ones truly responsible for the death of that little Susie Barnard."

"That was her name? Susie?"

"Yes, Joe. She had a name and a life to live that had barely begun." Bud was surprised at the emotion this fellow expressed, just in the way his shoulders drooped and the bow of his head.

Joe stood there, defeated, for several minutes. He did not move. Bud was patient. Finally, in a choked voice, Joe said, "There are a lot of boats that come into Montauk. I know you know that." He paused. "Some of them bring in more than fish, if you get my meaning."

Bud nodded. He did not want to interrupt.

"There's a guy at Gurney's, a big, heavy fellow. He kind of organizes things, I guess. I think his name is Greenburg...or Grunwald... John something..." Joe stopped quickly. "You did say you'd give me immunity?

"Yes, I did."

"All I know is that I get boxes delivered on a regular basis with the little packets – all ready for distribution, if you can call it that? It's that easy. I don't really know where they come from and who packages the stuff – the White Sugar...the Coke... and I don't ask."

"Any names?"

"Then there's a guy named Eldridge from the Inn. He's my contact... but he's not the fat guy."

"Who delivers the boxes to you?"

"Looks to be a kid from the kitchen – never the same person. The boxes come early in the morning, before the bar is even open. There's a call to me at home first, so I'm sure to be here at the bar to receive..."

"I have to thank you Joe for being so direct. This is enough for now. It's getting late and I'm sure you have to get back to business. Here's my card. I'll certainly be in touch again – and soon," and the two men turned and went inside.

As they shook hands at the door, Bud looked around the room. The place was buzzing as the drinks flowed and the decibel was high. He noticed the waitress in her short white apron with a bow at the back, her polished boots and mini skirt, and her bright red hair. "Hmm,' he thought. 'That's the dish.' She was bending over towards a craggy-faced fisherman who was eyeing her with lust. She was teasing him, flirting, even touching his hand. The poor old fellow was practically drooling.

What long legs she had!

As Bud left to go back to his car, he stopped cold in the street. NO! It couldn't be! She was dead, drowned. But there was something so familiar, although he had only seen the woman from the back.

Bud shook his head. 'No way', he thought, but in mid-stride he turned and walked back to Joe's Warm-Up Bar.

Through the smoky glass window he peered. He stood there for a long time. He saw the woman pass back and forth, bending and dipping between tables. Finally she moved towards him, and for one second, her face was in full view behind the window.

Their eyes met, only for a second, but it was enough. Hers widened in shock as she looked at Bud Rose through the grayish glass, and her mouth formed a round O.

'By God, it's she', he thought. 'She's dead, drowned! But no! It's Jillian Burns, resurrected', and his body broke out in a cold sweat.

The realization that this red haired gargoyle was mother of baby, Starfish, made Bud Rose sick to his stomach.

He leaned over and retched on the street. There was vomit on his shoes and his uniform. The legs of his pants were filthy.

Bud wasn't sure how he got home. He smelled of throw-up. He realized he was running away from a terrible truth. 'I should have gone right in and nabbed her there and then,' he thought to himself, but rationalized that, on seeing him through the window, she would probably have slipped out the back door of Joe's Warm-Up Bar and disappeared into the night.

To face Jillian! He was just not prepared. In fact, he was in shock that she was still alive. Besides, how could he have gone into that bar as Deputy Sheriff with filthy pants and smelling of vomit. These were the excuses he gave himself, but they hardly assuaged the guilty thought, 'Am I derelict in my duty for not grabbing her now?'

He just knew to drive fast. It was late when he arrived home in Remsenburg. Violet was asleep in their bed, Starfish in her crib in the adjacent large-closet room. All was silent, as, after showering, he crept in beside his wife.

The first thing he did in the morning was pick up Starfish. Still in his pajamas, he held her tight. Then looking into the face of the little girl, he tried to see if Jillian Burns' features were translated onto the sweet features of his daughter. He could see no resemblance and breathed a sigh of relief.

"You're so intent." Violet was watching her husband with Starfish in his arms. "Are you memorizing her face?" this said with a curious little smile

"Something like that," he muttered and laid the child back in her crib.

That Jillian was still alive was such a shocker for Bud Rose.

If she survived the car accident into the deep during the violence of the storm, ROSE, then surely, so must have Sasha. Was he in Montauk also?

Bud made the decision to not tell anyone yet of Jillian's re-emergence into the world of the living, nor the possibility of Sasha's doing the same. He wanted to be absolutely sure before getting Violet and her family involved. George Annas would probably be elated that his son – no matter how tainted – was still alive. The old man had aged visibly since he had learned of the drowning accident.

As for the rest of the Annas family, for Stella Burns, Jillian's mother, and especially for Violet, the news would be excruciating.

He must return to the scene. He must confront, and yes, he must pursue to the inevitable end. Donning a fresh uniform, kissing his wife and his daughter good morning and goodbye, Deputy Sheriff Bud Rose went out to his cruiser and prepared to do just that.

In Montauk!

Chapter Twenty-One

THE SEA STAR

Jillian/Scarlet was in a frozen panic. She dropped her tray of drinks as she gazed through the smoky window of Joe's Warm-Up bar into the eyes of Bud Rose, her former lover and father of the baby girl she called Rose Bud.

She left the tray and broken glass on the floor, stepping over the liquor that pooled the linoleum, and ran quickly to Joe's office in back of the bar. He was not there. He was busy circulating his barroom world, chatting up his customers.

Scarlet grabbed the phone off Joe's desk. She dialed Sasha/Alistair's number at his station at the entrance of The Montauk Yacht Club dining room. He quickly picked up.

"It's Bud," she whispered.

"Scarlet?"

"He was here," she said, voice rising.

"Bud Rose came into the bar?" Alistair's tone was level, but his body was ice cold. He paused, dead silence on the phone between the two. Then, "Did he see you?"

She nodded.

"Scarlet! Did he see you?"

"Through the window."

"Well, that's not so bad."

"It's worse. He recognized me!"

"What?"

"He knew it was me. He looked right through me and he saw that I recognized him. Oh, it was an awful moment – only a few seconds – but God, Sasha, he'll be coming back. I know it. And if he realizes I'm alive, he'll assume you are too."

"Jeezus," he muttered. "We gotta make plans. I'll be off here in a few minutes. It's after 10:00," he said, glancing at his watch. "Wait there. Tell Joe you don't feel good and that I'm coming to get you. Lay low, Jillian, and for God sake, pull yourself together."

She nodded again.

"Hey, are you there? Do you hear me?"

"Yes, Sasha, I hear you."

He rang off.

Jillian/Scarlett sank onto Joe's lounge chair where many a trick had been performed. She felt feverish and was fanning herself with a folder from Joe's desk. On the cover, she noticed a name: Sea Star – followed by the words 'Luke Erickson'. Inside the folder was the deed to Luke's boat.

Joe had told her Luke owed him 'a bunch of money' for his drugs. 'Hasn't paid in weeks...' She figured the deed was probably collateral.

Luke Erickson. His boat. Sea Star. And that ride Luke Erickson had been begging her to take with him. She paused. 'What a way to go,' she thought.

Scarlet straightened up. She added gloss to her lips, in Joe's back bathroom where she kept a supply of make-up for repairs after their sexual games. She fluffed her hair, pulled her mini-skirt high to reveal as much leg as possible and returned to the bar.

Luke was there. He had that familiar look of lust. She sauntered over to him and actually leaned against his arm, which rested on the bar.

"Hey, beautiful."

"Hey, Luke," she responded, licking her lips. "You lookin' fine tonight."

"You too, sweetheart."

"I wanted to ask you something."

"Anything," he said, turning to her.

"Do you remember when you asked me to go on your boat...you know, for a ride?"

"How could I forget," he said, his face lighting up.

"Well, how about it? I mean, I'm...ready...."

"You serious?" Luke was on his feet, grinning like an ape.

"Dead serious, Luke," she said with her best smile and another lick of her lips.

"When?" Luke was more than eager to consummate the deal of the moment and the dream and fantasy he held with a passion.

"How about tomorrow?" She was coy.

"You bet! No problem. Look, I know there's a weather watch out, but we can always go another day...any day...as long as you really mean it."

"Oh I do mean it, Luke...like right away. I don't mind a bumpy ride, if you get my meaning," Scarlet said with a little laugh. "Let's make it tomorrow. A few extra waves slapping the hull might make it more exciting."

Luke roared with laughter. "Scarlet, you sure are my kind of woman!"

He agreed to pick her up at 10:00 the next morning in front of Joe's Warm-Up Bar.

"Prepare yourself, baby. Prepare yourself good for the ride of your life," were Luke's last words to Scarlet as she left his side and quit the bar to wait outside for Sasha.

'Prepare yourself, Luke, for a big disappointment! But, baby, you are one hell of a means of escape!' were her final thoughts as she stood in the dark street. 'And where you drop me off, who cares? At least I'll be out of this town!'

Chapter Twenty-Two
ESCAPE PLANS

Jillian felt less trapped. She had chosen an escape. Luke's boat! It was Sasha who was deeply disturbed by the idea of Bud Rose bearing down on them.

"We've gotta pick up stakes," he exclaimed, when he collected her outside Joe's Warm-up that night. "And we can't tell anybody. That means no goodbyes, Scarlet. No last minute kiss off to your lover-boy boss," he said pointedly.

"You mean we just disappear?"

"We've done it before."

By the next morning, they knew they had to separate, travel by different routes.

"Luke would never understand your being on his boat. He has no idea of you," Jillian said as she brushed the red hair and slipped into a short, swingy dress with a zipper down the front, and boots, of course, to compliment.

"Understood," Sasha replied as he pulled down the old canvas bag to pack their few things.

She gazed out the cabin window. "God, it's pouring!" she wailed.

"Well, expect to get wet, old girl. At least Luke can drop you somewhere up island."

"Yeah, but how will I tell the old guy I want to get off?"

"That's your problem. You'll think of something, Scarlet," he said sarcastically.

They were on the very tip of the landmass that was Long Island. Sasha and she had determined to make their separate ways to Stella Burns home in East Moriches, Jillian's mother's house, where both could feel relatively safe, at least for a moment.

"She'd never turn us in. I know my mother. Even with all her disgust at the two of us, she's loyal. Always has been." Jillian's words were rueful.

"I hope your right," Sasha responded. "But, we can only stay there for a day or two because you know Bud Rose will contact her, now that he knows you're alive."

"Mom doesn't even know yet that we didn't die in that storm. She's gonna be shocked." Jillian started to cry. "Where shall we go from there?"

"We'll cross that bridge. We'll tell your mother we're headed for New York City. She'll believe it and tell Bud Rose. For now, let's get a move on. I'll drop you in front of Joe's Warm-Up and you can wait for Luke and his precious boat. I'll take off west on Montauk Highway."

Sasha was still packing their small belongings in the soft bag. "I'll probably pass the good Deputy Sheriff on the highway – driving east to catch us both in Montauk," he said with a laugh. "Pretty ironic. At least he won't recognize the old green Chevy driving west with me in it."

"You've got transportation, but what about me? How am I supposed to get to East Moriches?" Jillian was suddenly angry.

"Keep staying alive! Staying alive," Sasha was singing as he packed. "You'll have to leave some of these boots behind. Sorry, Jillian, Can't be helped," he said, noticing the sour turn to her mouth.

"Sasha! Stop it. How am I going to get to East Moriches?"

"When you hit land and get off Luke's boat, either get a train or hire a taxi to drive you there. Call your Mom. Tell her I'm on my way and that you are too."

"You're certainly nonchalant about all this."

"I've got some money. Here." Sasha handed her a wad of bills. "Hey you've got money too. You're loaded. All those White Sugar tips! Ah, stop looking like you're about to start crying again." Sasha went to her and put his arm around her shoulders.

"I'm scared, Sasha," she sniveled.

"You'll be fine," he said, patting her. "Just put on some of that Scarlet charm, and there'll be no problem, even if you and Luke have to come back here to Montauk."

"Why would we have to?"

"Weather maybe?"

"What if Bud's around?"

"You have to pray he won't be. In any case, just go to the train station and head west."

With that, Sasha left the key to the cabin on the coffee table in the living area, grabbed the canvas bag with one hand and Jillian's arm in the other and went out the door. "Goodbye Hither Hills," he said jauntily, as he put the car in gear and headed off to Montauk proper.

At almost exactly the same time, Bud Rose was driving from Remsenburg on Montauk Highway east toward the hamlet. He was eager to interrogate Joe of the Warm-Up Bar, and hopefully —although with some trepidation – interrogate the redheaded Jillian about the drug traffic in which the two were involved.

Bud never noticed an old green Chevy driving fast enough to spray his car with puddled water. He never saw it pass, because it was a dreadful, rainy morning, dark, ominous. However, the road was clear and he made decent time, arriving shortly before noon, just as the bar was opening. Little did he know that had he arrived perhaps an hour earlier, he would have seen Jillian/Scarlet standing outside the door of Joe's Warm-Up, awaiting the arrival of Luke Erickson.

What a near miss. A whole different scenario would have been enacted, had Bud arrived in the nick of time and seen his re-headed ex-lover tapping her foot.

Chapter Twenty-Three

THE SMELLY SLICKER

Jillian/Scarlet was waiting outside of Joe's Warm-Up Bar on that rainy, late October mid-morning for Luke Erickson to arrive. She felt queasy at the thought of the roiling sea. Her last encounter with it had been near disaster. However, she had made peace with herself realizing, for her, Luke's boat was the best means of eluding Bud Rose. She was positive Bud would be on her tail immediately.

She was right.

Luke arrived after a few minutes. With a big smile, he got out of his truck and approached her.

"Hey, Scarlet. You sure you want to do this? Going to be a bit rough out there." She noticed he smelled of aftershave. He wore clean trousers and a checked shirt.

"Of course, Luke. Why not?"

"You're quite a dame," he announced proudly and threw a smelly slicker over her shoulders to protect against the increasingly heavy raindrops. "Let's be off to the Sea Star!"

"Sea Star," she exclaimed. "What a great name."

"Yeah, it's for luck. In the fisherman's world, a sea star – really a starfish – brings the waves under control and a gigantic catch of fish in the nets. Or so they say," he said with a laugh. "Don't know if it's true, but a bit of luck always helps."

"You can say that again," Scarlet said with a wry smile.

In his truck, they went through the side streets of Montauk, Jillian/

Scarlet looking through the window wistfully. 'Probably I'll never see Montauk again,' she thought. 'Been quite a time here. Joe...now Luke?' She looked at her driver. God, he looked old, leathery, but kind of sweet. She leaned against his shoulder.

That pleased him. "Looks like the wind's picking up. "Probably be pretty bouncy out there. Hope you like bouncy?"

"I love bouncy, Luke."

"Me too." He was alive with anticipation.

The Sea Star was anchored at the wharf on the bay side of Montauk. It was a typical fishing boat, with large cabin, a small crane for hauling nets, a tangle of equipment at the prow. There was a small stove with a black coffee percolator atop, and a flat cot with a tired-looking blanket covering it in the cockpit. The controls were up front.

Luke led Scarlet into the cabin. She sat down on the straight chair behind a small battened-down table for eating purposes or writing notes, she assumed. She could feel the boat rising and falling quite uncontrollably, as Luke went outside to cast off.

The whole place smelled of fish.

"Have I made a huge mistake?" she muttered to herself. "Where the hell am I going to end up?"

The fisherman returned He was rubbing his hands. "We'll move out to the bay, Miss Scarlet, and then get down to business."

'Uh oh,' she thought. "Was it just for luck you named your boat Sea Star?" she asked, to deflect his amorous thoughts.

"Luck – I guess so. But I've always loved sea stars. As a kid, I remember, sometimes at a full moon, when the moon was really dazzling and hitting on the ocean, a starfish would jump out of the water and fall back down...as if the light of the moon had forced it to leap."

"Magical," she said.

"Yeah. Starfish can regenerate lost arms – can regrow an entire limb. Did you know that?"

Scarlet shook her head. "Like a phoenix from the ashes." "Oooh," she shrieked. A huge wave had hit the Sea Star, tilting it to one side.

"Told you it'd be bouncy!" Luke said with a laugh. "That was nothing."

"That was nothing?" she said, her stomach churning.

"Hey, whatever the ocean wants, the ocean gets."

""You sound like it's alive."

"Oh, it is," he said firmly.

"I hope it doesn't get us!" With that, another wave tilted the boat to the other side. "God, Luke."

He was standing at the front of the cockpit with the helm-wheel in his hands. "Should be getting a little less rough – maybe in a few minutes – then lady, I want you on that cot."

"What?"

"You heard me, Scarlet. What'd you think I brought you here for? A ride in the rain?" His tone was ugly.

"Ah, come on, Luke. We barely know each other."

"Well, it's time we did …know each other… real well…real intimately," he said. "I mean <u>real</u> intimately!" and he gave a harsh laugh.

Another tremendous wave hit the front of the boat, splashing the front window with water, beading it so it was hard to see. Scarlet shrieked again.

"I love the sound of that," Luke said. "I expect to hear a lot of your yelping on that cot."

"Look, I think I may throw up. I feel really sick," she said, staggering to her feet. "Is there a john?"

"In the corner," he growled.

Scarlet found the small water closet and closed the door. She did not throw up, but sat on the toilet, gathering her thoughts as the boat rocked up and down.

"Luke. I'm sick," she called through the door. "Please – let's go back to Montauk. This was a horrible mistake."

"You can say that again!" he yelled back angrily and with a great swerve, she felt the boat turning. She sat there on the toilet, bouncing up and down, until she felt the boat hit something and heard the motor die.

Chapter Twenty-Four
NOT SO WARM-UP

"We're not open yet," Joe yelled as he heard a tap on the door of the bar. "Wait until noon." He was placing a cardboard box on the floor behind the bar.

The tap on the door continued, louder, persistent.

"What the hell," Joe muttered as he crossed over to the front door. "Oh, it's you," he remarked on seeing the tall figure of Deputy Sheriff Bud Rose standing in the rain. He let the officer in. "You're back? Already?"

"Yeah, Joe. I have some real concerns, questions. You knew I'd be coming down to Montauk."

"Yeah. I expected you, but maybe not so soon. Anyway, come on back to my office."

Bud followed Joe into the room behind the bar.

"So what do you want to know? Wanta cup of coffee?"

"Sure. Black."

Joe poured two cups from the Mister Coffee machine placed on a shelf near the window. He handed one to Bud, then sat in his lounge chair, taking a large sip from his cup. Bud stood before him, looking straight at him.

"You told me you receive a regular box of packets of smack through Mr. Eldridge over at Gurney's Inn. Is that right?"

Joe nodded. "Yeah, Every couple of weeks. In fact one came already this morning. It's on the floor behind the bar."

"Really! You told me that Eldridge is your contact, but he's a small fish. Who supplies HIM? Would you know?"

Joe nodded again.

"Well?"

"It's that guy – big rich – who has a suite there. I think he recently bought a house at Culloden Point. Anyway, he's basically a New Yorker – owns some big buildings - supposedly a mover and shaker. I've only seen him twice by chance. He's a heavy guy. I think his name is Grunwald."

'Bingo!' Bud thought. "And why do you think he's involved in drug trafficking?"

"He's got a yacht. Keeps it at Gurney's. Eldridge told me that the boat goes out every week – without Grunwald but with a very tough crew. They come back into the long wharf there and deliver the packets to Eldridge who then has one of his minions bring the stuff over here – and probably delivers to other places too. But that I don't know for sure."

"So Grunwald's the big shot in this deal. You sure?"

"Yeah, I'm sure." Joe bowed his head, ashamed. "I should have told you before, but he's a scary guy."

"What do you mean?"

"Power. Connections. Drug dealing is no easy profession!"

"Yeah. It's a lethal business," Bud said. "But you have no doubt Grunwald's the top banana?"

"None."

Bud had moved away from Joe in his lounge chair. He was over near the window with his back to him. Over his shoulder, he asked, "And the red-haired waitress? What is her part in this little game?"

"Scarlet?"

"That's her name, Scarlet?"

"Yeah. She's new. Been working for me since early in the summer. She's kind of sassy. The customers like her."

"That's not what I'm asking."

"I know. I know. She delivers the packets and takes the cash for it with the tab and brings it to me. She gets $100 a pop."

"That's a pretty good deal for her, Joe."

"You bet. But she's straight with me and I'm straight with her. We have a little extra 'arrangement' on the side…" Joe said with a nasty little laugh.

"What do you mean?"

"Oh, it's not monetary. It has to do with - shall we say- major bodily functions."

"Oh, I see." Bud could just imagine the long legs of Scarlet/Jillian entwining this man as they had often entwined him, in another life. "What time does she get here for work?

"Around 5:00 o'clock. But hey, officer. She's really only in it for the dough. Doesn't use. Neither do I. Go easy on her."

Bud made no comment. Then, he said, "I'll leave you for now. But I'll be back around 5:00. Do me a favor and don't tell Scarlet I'm coming, okay?"

"Okay. Hey, you did promise me immunity!"

"I sure did. I'll honor that. You might get probation or a fine."

"What?"

"Depends on the judge. You know I'll put in a good word."

Joe looked sullen.

"You've been a good citizen to report this stuff, Joe, but you must know, that I'll have to shut you down..."

"What? My bar?"

"No, no. You're bar can stay open. But you'll have to close off one of your services."

Joe looked crestfallen.

"No more White Sugar," were Bud's last words as he made his way out to the street.

In his cruiser, the Deputy Sheriff took out his notebook and Bic pen. His list:

1. Grunwald
2. Eldridge
3. Bethany Brandeis, Realtor for Culloden Point property for Grunwald?
4. Interrogate Jillian – 5:00pm – Sasha?
5. Call Stella Burns, J.'s mother
6. See Montauk police – a substation of East Hampton Police Dept. On Embassy Street in Montauk

He sat for a minute, then, with raindrops sloshing the vehicle and wind beating its sides, Bud Rose, Deputy Sheriff headed over to Gurney's Inn.

"I think I'll order one of their specialties," he said aloud. "That lobster roll."

Chapter Twenty-Five

NAPEAGUE

Scarlet found herself unceremoniously dumped in mushy reeds. She had no idea that she was on the coastline of the tiny hamlet of Napeague, a sparsely occupied strip of land between the Atlantic Ocean and Gardiner's Bay to the north, and to the east of Hither Hills State Park.

Napeague was the place where Luke said his final farewell with a sarcastic, "Nice knowing you, Scarlet. You're a nasty little bitch. Good riddance."

With a toot of the whistle, Sea Star and its captain, springing up and down on the swelling waves, left her standing there in the marsh next to the bay. She watched through the rain until the boat was out of view.

Soaked to the skin, for a moment she wished for Luke's smelly slicker. That was absolutely all she wanted of him! 'What a gentleman. NOT!' she thought. She was relieved to be rid of him and was thankful to be out of Montauk proper. Bud could never find her here.

Wherever here was! Looking at her wet body, she thought with a laugh. 'not only Bud couldn't find me, but nobody else could either.'

Shrugging her shoulders, always resourceful, Jillian managed to climb the wet hillock and found herself near what looked to be a private marine fish hatchery. Next to it was a lighted building with the sign, Sea Slug Lounge.

"Aha!" she said aloud. "At least I have cash! From now on, I'm back to Jillian Burns. No more Scarlet!" and with a sigh, she set off for the Sea Slug Lounge.

The Sea Slug! Jillian found it a most appropriate name considering her bedraggled state. When she entered, she found a venue almost as bedraggled as she. The place was empty but for a woman of a certain age behind the bar, and an elderly couple at a table in the corner of a dim, wooden room. The two were nursing beers.

There were trophies on the walls – stuffed fish of various sorts – and the place smelled of old cigarettes and spilled booze, but it was dry. For that, Jillian was thankful.

"Hey, you look drowned," the woman called from her post among the liquor bottles. "Come on in." She came forward to Jillian with a towel. "Here, rub yourself off."

"Gee, thanks," Jillian said. "It sure is wet out there. By the way, where am I?"

"Where are you?" The woman looked startled. "Hey, you all right?" You're at The Sea Slug."

"I know. I know. But I mean, what town?"

"Napeague. You know, we're not far from Amagansett, East Hampton."

"Can a get a train from…"

"Either one. I guess Amagansett Station is nearest. Where you goin? And how'd you get here? And by the way, do you want a drink?"

"I'd love something hot."

"Coffee? I have tea."

"Ah, tea. Nothing in it. Just tea. That'd be great." The woman went to fetch a cup. Returning with it, she remarked, "You just come from out of nowhere…"

"I had a fight with my boy friend. He threw me off his boat," Jillian said as she sat at a table, cup in front of her.

The woman laughed. "That's not very nice, and in this weather."

"No, HE's not very nice," Jillian said, laughing too. She took a sip. "Thanks for this," she said. "Is there any way I can get to the station?"

"Well, my son will be along soon. He's the regular bartender here. He could drive you."

"I'll pay him, of course."

"He'd expect no less," the woman said with a smile. "By the way, I'm Susanna. I'm the owner of The Sea Slug."

"You've been most kind, Susanna. Is there a phone I could use? Want to call my mom. Let her know I'm alive."

"Sure. Over there."

"Mom?"

"Hello? Hello?" There was a pause. "Who is this?" said with a cautious tone.

"It's me, Mom."

There was dead silence. Jillian then heard a small crash as if the phone receiver had fallen. She waited, alarmed. Had her mother keeled over?

"Jillian?" There was a sob in the voice.

"Yes, Mom. It's really me. I'm sorry ---it must be such a shock to hear my voice, to know that I'm not dead. I'm very much alive."

There was a long pause. "Where are you?"

"Napeague. It's near Montauk – a tiny town."

"Napeague? Montauk? Have you been there all this time? How did you survive that awful storm? They found your car in the surf... It was last spring... months ago." There was a pause. "You never called...never let me know..."

"I know. I know. It's a long story. I'll fill you in as soon as I get home."

"You're coming here?"

"Yes, if that's okay with you."

"Oh, Jillian, my wayward daughter. Yes, of course. After all, you're flesh and blood. Why didn't you call?"

Jillian did not answer, then "Sasha will be coming too. He'll be arriving separately."

"Sasha!"

"Yeah. He survived the storm too, of course."

"Jill, he's bad news."

"I know, but he helped me a lot. I kind of owe him."

"What about the cops? Are they still after you two?"

"Yep. 'Fraid so. And I'm sure Deputy Sheriff Bud Rose will be calling you. He saw me just a couple of days ago– recognized me – knows I'm still around. He'll probably want to let you know I'm alive and kicking."

"I haven't heard anything."

"Well, if you do, please act surprised…"

"That won't be hard," Stella Burns said with a snort.

"Just play dumb. You have no idea I survived and no idea where I could be. You got it?"

"I got it, Jill." Jillian could hear a quiet sob in her mother's voice. "How long before you get here?"

"Can't say. I'm hoping to get a train east. When I know the time I get to the Speonk train station, I'll give you a call and maybe you can pick me up?"

"Of course. I hope no one sees you there."

"Me too."

"Be careful, Jill. I can't wait for you to come… you're alive…" Stella could not continue.

"Don't worry, Mom." Jillian paused. "Hey I want to ask you something."

"Fire away."

"Have you seen…the baby? Rose Bud?" Jillian's voice was almost inaudible.

"Yes. I have. Violet has brought her here a couple of times."

"And? Are they taking good care…?"

"Oh, yes. They love her. She is really precious. By the way, they do not call her Rose Bud. They call her – of all things – Starfish."

"Starfish?"

"It's their pet name for her. They say a starfish is good luck. Violet is a wonderful mother and Bud – well, he just dotes on that baby." Stella Burns' voice had grown warm.

Jillian could not speak. Finally she said, "See you soon, Mom," and, as she hung up, wiped away a tear with the back of her hand.

Chapter Twenty-Six
MARTIN ELDRIDGE

Bud was just finishing the lobster roll inside the Gurney's Inn Bar and Grill when he saw Martin Eldridge enter the small restaurant. He was wearing a damp raincoat and his sandy hair was wet. He came right over to Bud and said, "They told me you were here. You want to speak with me?"

"I do, Mr. Eldridge. I have a few questions involving a case I'm working on where you might be of help."

"Glad to be of service," the Inn manager said with a benign little smile. He removed the coat, shaking it, folding it, placing it on an empty chair beside Bud's table.

"Would you like a coffee?" Bud asked.

"Good idea."

Bud signaled a waiter, ordered two coffees, as Eldridge said to the young man, "please put this on my chit."

"That's not necessary," Bud remarked.

"Am I bribing a policeman?" Eldridge quipped, trying to lighten whatever questions were to come.

'Boy, this man is one nervous little fellow,' Bud was thinking. "I'm afraid a cup of coffee wouldn't do it," Bud said. "But let me get down to serious business...why I'm here."

"Please do."

The coffee had arrived. Each man took a sip as if to prepare himself.

"Is there a gentleman here by the name of Grunwald?" Bud had taken out his notebook. He was looking down but was fully aware of the expressions on Eldridge's face. The man had gone quite pale and his upper lip twitched.

"Mr. Grunwald? Why, yes. He is one of our regulars. John Grunwald. Has a large permanent suite here. Just bought a house just outside of Montauk so I don't know how long he'll keep the place at the Inn." Eldridge paused. "Why?"

"Why what?"

"Why do you want to know about Mr. Grunwald. He's very well known in New York City – Real Estate. Very important. Very rich." Eldridge was babbling.

"I understand he keeps a yacht here."

Well, not exactly here – but close enough. It's huge!"

"Does he use it often?"

"Oh, I wouldn't know that. Look, I should be getting back to my desk…if that's all…"

"It's not all. I have a few more questions, Mr. Eldridge. Like how well do you know Joe, of Joe's Warm-Up Bar?"

"Who?" The man's face had turned quite pink.

"Joe… his last name is Grady. He owns that bar off Main Street."

"Oh, that Joe."

"Yes. That Joe."

"Well, it's really not my kind of place."

"Yet you manage to deliver a packing box to that 'place' on a pretty regular basis, now don't you?"

"What?"

"You send one of your minions over to Joe's Warm-Up Bar twice a month – early in the morning – with a box full of packets of White Sugar isn't that right?"

"I don't know what you're talking about. If that Joe person said I did that – it's his word against mine. I'm going to have to leave you now…"

"I don't think so, Mr. Eldridge. I'm afraid you're coming with me." Bud Rose stood up and threw a few dollar bills on the table. "Come on now."

Martin Eldridge just sat there in shock.

"You don't want me to handcuff you."

"No. No, certainly not. I have nothing to hide," he said, gathering up his coat.

The two men left the Gurney's Inn Bar and Grill, walking slowly through the lobby and out to Bud's cruiser.

In the front seat, as Bud placed the vehicle in gear, Martin Eldridge turned to the Deputy Sheriff and asked, "Is this absolutely necessary, officer?"

"What? Are you thinking of bribing me again," Bud said with a twinkle. "I'm afraid it is necessary, Mr. Eldridge. Absolutely necessary."

The car moved forward and made its way, through the town to The East Hampton Town Police Department – substation Montauk.

He left Martin Eldridge there in the custody of two policemen and arranged to have him transported by van the next day (with Jillian if he found her) to the Riverhead office where Bud himself would take depositions.

And Sasha?

Ah! Maybe Sasha too. That would be a coup – but still, small fish.

John Grunwald was out there…big, formidable, and probably lethal. After all, drug barons do not go easy into that good night.

Chapter Twenty-Seven

VANISHED

"Dammit, Joe!" Bud was furious, frustrated. "Did you warn her I was coming back?"

"No. I swear I didn't. Haven't seen her. She's never late - always right on time – right on the button - five o'clock."

It was now 6:30 PM.

"Where does she live?"

"In a cabin at Bayview of Hither Hills Park – with her husband. His name is Alistair."

"Her husband?" Bud's antenna went up. "What's he look like?"

"I don't know…kind of British – thin moustache – graying hair…"

"Old?"

"No, no. Just gone gray early, I guess. Scarlet doesn't seem to be that 'into' him."

"Scarlet! I love it."

"That's her name. Scarlet Williams from Teaneck, New Jersey."

Bud burst out laughing. "Well, you know what?"

"What's to laugh at?"

"Your Scarlet Williams is really Jillian Burns from Westhampton Beach."

"Huh?"

"Yep. And Joe, she was involved in an automobile theft ring. I was on her tail for months until the storm, ROSE, last May. Her getaway car was found overturned in the surf. No bodies were ever found – her or her…husband?" Bud laughed again. "Husband!"

"God."

"Yep, our Jillian. 'Course she didn't have short red hair. She didn't wear boots and low cut blouses. Oh no. Not our Jillian – she was the receptionist at the Sheriff's office in Westhampton Beach."

"You've gotta be kidding."

"No. It's the truth. I recognized her last night… saw her through the front window as I left your bar. Should have come in and picked her up then. She's probably well on her way out of Montauk by now, damn it."

"I know they had a car…an old green Chevy."

Bud was kicking himself mentally. He felt remiss in not fulfilling his policeman's duty. The woman had gotten away again – and so had 'Alistair'. Bud was sure the 'husband' Scarlet professed to have was none other than Sasha. How had the two escaped the turmoil of ROSE? How had they arrived safe and sound here in Montauk? 'It's a puzzlement,' he thought.

"And the fat guy Grunwald? How big is his involvement here?" Bud probed Joe about the mysterious tycoon.

"Don't know much…don't know him at all, but my guess is he's plenty involved…probably in deep."

"Really." Bud waited. He wanted more about the man, but it did not come. "Well, there's not much point in my hanging around here, Joe. I'll leave you to your business out front. But no more packets! In fact, I'm going to confiscate the box you got through Eldridge. Evidence."

Joe said nothing.

"Hey, I appreciate your cooperation, Joe. You know that."

"Immunity?" Joe questioned.

"Certainly. Your assistance will be considered seriously by any judge – with my word along with it. By the way, do you know if that Alistair guy had a job?"

"Yeah. He was *Maitre'd* over at The Montauk Yacht Club…the main dining room."

"Good Lord!" Bud exclaimed. "Did he peddle the White Sugar too – along with Scarlet?"

"Don't know for sure… but probably. Scarlet always asked for packets to take home for hubby to sell. She always brought back the money to me. I never asked her directly, though, if it was he who sold them or her."

Bud stood up. He had been perched on Joe's lounger in the back room of the bar. Joe was standing by the window.

"I'd best be going. Now, sir, would you be good enough to hand over that box? Please?"

Joe went to a closet next to the bathroom, reached in and retrieved the cardboard box from the floor and handed it over to Bud.

"You're doing the right thing, Joe."

"As if I had a choice…"

Bud laughed. "Look, you're a lot better off than Mr. and Mrs. Alistair Williams –that IS the name they're using - of Teaneck, New Jersey, yet? Those two are going to be doing some real time. Your cooperation is going to pay off for you, when this whole drug business comes down."

"It better. Whatever you say, officer … that is if you catch them," Joe added, as he led Bud Rose through the bar, which was as noisy with half-inebriated patrons as ever, and out onto the street.

"We'll be in touch," Bud said.

"No doubt," the bar owner replied and turned on his heel and re-entered his place of business, head down, knowing that without White Sugar, his income would take a huge hit…but at least, no jail, please God!

Before going to the Montauk Police Substation to drop off the evidence, the box of packets of smack, Bud made a stop at The Montauk Yacht Club.

He went directly to the main dining room and was told by a distraught captain of waiters, that the *Maitre' d*, Alistair Williams, had not shown up for work, that he left the staff to labor overtime, that he, the captain, had double duties, and where was the damn fool?

"Okay. Okay," Bud said. "Calm down. I'm sure he'll show up in due course."

"Maybe. Never did trust that man…something phony about him. He'll never show up tonight! I just know he is gone for good…and good riddance!" and the captain disappeared in a flurry.

"No," Bud murmured. "Not tonight, for sure."

Bud went out to the cruiser. He sat for a while in the front seat. 'Now what?' he thought, as he finally started the engine to drive over to the Montauk Police substation. He planned to give them the box of evidence to go in the van tomorrow with Eldridge to The Riverhead Sheriff's Office. Aloud, he blurted out into the darkness, "I'd better call Stella Burns. I wonder if Jillian will go there. At least Stella should know her daughter isn't dead!"

In the next days, Bud planned to take the formal deposition from Eldridge and prepare what evidence they had for trial. He hoped to get more information from the Inn manager about the top dog – the heavy set man who seemed to be calling the shots.

John Grunwald.

Chapter Twenty-Eight

THE DEAL MAKER

John Grunwald, magnate from New York City, had decided that ownership of the house near Culloden Point was a solid investment. He had made a good deal with Brandeis Realty at The Circle in Montauk. He appreciated owning a piece of land and a glamorous house. He liked the whole Montauk area because many famous events and people had been part of it. John Grunwald liked famous. In fact, he loved famous. Culloden Point was named after a British ship that ran aground in 1781 while pursuing a French frigate. To keep it from falling into enemy hands, the crew threw the cannons overboard and burned the ship.

Also, Grunwald's ego was inflated because The Montauk Lighthouse – so near by – was the first public works project of the new United States, authorized by President George Washington in 1792, and finally lit in 1797. Being so close to that flame, made John Grunwald feel important. And Montauk County Park, where, in 1898, Theodore Roosevelt's Rough Riders recovered from yellow fever and typhoid after the Spanish American War, was close. Being surrounded by the aura of such famous persons made John Grunwald's ego puff up like a large balloon. He felt just as famous - as if he was among his peers, and that he belonged there.

He had always enjoyed his suite at Gurney's Inn, but it was a public place, where he would often see friends and business associates, encounters he did not seek nor relish. His house on Culloden Point provided him the privacy he demanded, and frankly, needed.

John Grunwald, in his black suit – even on hot summer days – with the overlong red power tie – was, *au fond*, a secretive man. In spite of an expansive, embracing personality, underneath, John Grunwald was dark and given to misogyny and malfeasance. He loved money more than anything in life.

The man had found a resource far more lucrative than any buildings he could build and sell, namely narcotics.

With certain connections in New York City, and the access to drugs from the boats off of Montauk, John Grunwald, over a period of two years, had become the head honcho of a very lucrative cartel.

The suite at the Inn had been sufficient early on, but now that business had grown to such an extent, it seemed prudent to find a place among the bushes, out of the way and hidden. Culloden Point.

With hair that looked bleached, a bloated face, and fake tan, (he hated the sun), John Grunwald still managed to attract women. He had been divorced twice. No children. Never wanted any.

But, oh he was rich! That forgave a lot, to a certain kind of female. Also, on his best behavior, he could be courtly. That helped the medicine go down – that, with a little extra red wine and the possibility of an expensive gift –made a sexual romp at least feasible for an ambitious girl.

In his lair at Culloden Point, on that late October afternoon in 1985, John Grunwald had learned within minutes that The Gurney's Inn manager, Martin Eldridge, had been led off by a Deputy Sheriff. The receptionist at the Inn was well aware of the secret drug machinations that took place there. She had phoned Grunwald to warn him of the arrest, being no fool and knowing where the goodies lay. She was sure he would appreciate her notifying him, hopefully in an expensive way.

John Grunwald immediately called his chauffeur who brought his Mercedes to the front door of the house on Culloden Point, and the tycoon was off to Manhattan and his apartment in Trump Tower on Fifth Avenue.

When he arrived at his palatial digs, (and they were grand and new, the building having been opened only two years earlier), he ordered up a steak dinner with all the fixings, from the Grill downstairs, and then, booked a flight to Paris for the following morning, First Class, of course.

He next called The Hotel Crillon in that loveliest of cities and secured a suite for an indeterminate number of days. He was well known at The Crillon. His generosity and largesse were greatly appreciated by the staff. He knew he would be welcomed.

John Grunwald also made several calls to associates in the narcotics business, telling them that he would be out of the country for a period, that the Long Island police were sniffing around in a very real way, and that they should lay low for the time being.

The last phone conversations made him feel strangely deprived, depleted. He felt hungry, and ordered, again from the Grill, his favorite dessert: its double chocolate cake with two scoops of vanilla ice cream.

John Grunwald then phoned Richard Willis, the Captain of his yacht, named *The Otellia*, ordering him to sail the boat to a private marina in Connecticut where it could be moored for a few months. Grunwald's sister, Melinda, had property in Mystic and a boat of her very own, but not nearly so lavish as John's. Yet, hers was still, a handsome sea craft.

Once moored at Mystic Marina, and presumably safe, John Grunwald promised Captain Willis a well-earned vacation. After all, the man had brought in a lot of smack to the wharf at Gurney's Inn on *The Otellia*. The Captain would now have several weeks to enjoy himself, while his boss figured out the next steps.

John Grunwald was frank with his Captain, had employed him for several years. He explained that Gurney's Inn would now be off limits to the trade, particularly that long wharf at the end of Gurney's beach where "White Sugar was unloaded and injected into the community." Other arrangements would have to be made, but of course, "not to worry." He, John Grunwald, would take care of everything "as I always do!"

"You know me, my Captain. We'll be back in business soon, I promise. Trust me," were his words on the phone to his employee. As he hung up, John Grunwald took a long look at himself in a mirror on the wall opposite the small dining table at which he sat. The piece of furniture was made with a gold-leaf finish. "For a man going on 70, I don't look so bad," he said out loud to his image in the mirror, brushing back the bleached hair with his hand. "Not so bad at all. I'll see what Paris has to offer, something sweet with big breasts, something sexy," and with that, he finished off the last of his vanilla ice cream.

Chapter Twenty-Nine

JILLIAN CONFIRMED!

Before Bud Rose headed back to Remsenburg, that frustrating final night in the month of October, he went to The Bayview of Hither Hills Park and spoke to the owner of the little complex, which was made up of old tourist cabins, refitted and cheap.

"Yes, the Williams left just today - before the end of their lease," the fellow said. "So abruptly!"

"Can I see inside their cabin?" Bud flashed his badge. "Has the place been cleaned yet?"

"No, the girl comes in tomorrow," the owner said, opening the door to cabin #5.

Bud looked around the meager rooms carefully. From the bathroom, he took a wet washcloth, (for DNA), a depleted bottle of gray hair dye, and a small, empty make-up case with the initials JB on the cover. He recognized it, had seen it before on Jillian Burn's bed table in her apartment near King Kullen when Bud and she had been sexual partners.

"Jillian!" This cinched it for him, this personal item he had seen her use – so often –"for repairs after the loving, Rose Bud," she would coo at him. How he had hated that appellation.

He continued looking for the Williams' leftovers. In the closet, on the floor, he found two sets of women's patent leather boots, one pair in black, the other red. These he also confiscated.

There was nothing else.

In the cruiser, as he drove along Montauk Highway toward Hampton Bays and finally Remsenburg and his home, he decided it best to go to East Moriches and speak to Stella Burns in person. He would drive up there the next day.

Now that he was positive Scarlet Williams from Teaneck, New Jersey – the name brought a smile to his lips – was indeed Jillian, it was incumbent upon him to do the right thing about her mother.

'The woman will be stunned,' he thought. "God! Her daughter Jillian who she thought drowned, is still alive!" this burst from his lips.

And Violet?

How was he going to tell his wife that the biological mother of his daughter, beloved little Starfish, was still of this world, that the ocean had not taken her to its bosom. Somehow, Jillian, and Sasha, (Violet's own brother), had escaped, first the violent ocean waves, and then, Bud's policeman's grasp.

"First the ocean let them free…and now I let …" Bud hit the wheel with the back of his hand. "What a klutz," he yelled out. "I should have taken Jillian in that first night when I saw her…should have gone back to the bar and arrested her…"

He groaned. "And how in hell am I ever going to explain to Violet that Starfish's mother may come looking for her baby, Rose Bud?"

It was hard, very hard. Bud sat his wife down in the living room of the house at the end of Shore Road. Violet was in a night shirt, having been roused from bed by her husband who drew her by the hand into the darkened family room and sat her down on the couch beside him.

A triangle of light from the half-open bedroom door was the only way he could see her face, which slowly crumpled before his eyes as his story unfolded.

Bud's voice was soft, as he described Jillian in her Scarlet Williams from Teaneck, New Jersey role - with her red hair and thigh-high boots. He told Violet of the woman's toughness, of how she had escaped the ocean's might during the storm, ROSE, of her living with Violet's brother,

Sasha, in a cabin at The Bayview of Hither Hills Park near Montauk, and that she worked in a bar.

"Did you speak with her?"

"No. I should have arrested her when I first recognized her. But I didn't."

Bud got to his feet. "God, I regret that I didn't take her in then and there. And now she's off and running... probably with Sasha in tow."

"Sasha's alive." It was a statement. "At least, Dad will be happy about that," Violet said, her voice almost inaudible. "Oh, Bud, what does it mean? What does it mean for Starfish?"

It was a question he dreaded. He composed himself, and parrying her worry, his voice tender, said "It shouldn't mean anything, Violet. Look. Jillian is a wanted fugitive. She was before ROSE, over that car theft business, and she is now. I didn't mention that at the bar where she worked, she was pushing smack."

"Smack?"

"Dope."

Violet was silent. Then she rose and crossed the room to Bud. She stood before him. In her bare feet, she only came up to his shoulder. Looking up in her husband's face, she asked, "Starfish, Bud? Does Jillian have any claim...could she...?"

"No, no, darling," he replied, taking her in his arms. "She's a wanted fugitive. Jillian will do time, once I catch her. Don't worry, Violet. She has no claim. Never will."

"I pray not," Violet sighed. "But never?"

Bud felt her tears against his chest.

Chapter Thirty
STELLA BURNS

Bud Rose left early the next morning. The sky was overcast and gray. He was on his way to the East Moriches house of Stella Burns with the dubious task of informing her of her daughter's reappearance on this earth. He had to tell her that Jillian was very much alive and in deeper trouble than before the presumed fatal accident in the surf off Dune Road during the storm, ROSE.

He thought it more than possible that Jillian had already called her mother – but with that one, it was impossible to know what to expect. It was also conceivable that Jillian had actually gone to East Moriches and was there in her mother's house.

In any case, Bud expected the confrontation with Stella Burns to be short and hopefully without too much drama. From there, the Deputy Sheriff, was headed into New York City and the NYPD to report certain accusations made and certain evidence gathered (from Eldridge) against a man named John Grunwald.

Bud knew Grunwald was well known in Manhattan. A flamboyant realtor and man-about-town, with a spread at Trump Tower close to Central Park, Grunwald was a ribald icon of the city. To Bud Rose, information about Grunwald's possible drug connections and possible devious behavior in terms of his yacht, *The Otellia*, needed to be made available to the city police department.

In other words, Bud Rose needed help, but first things first.

Bud arrived at Stella Burn's modest home in East Moriches near 10:00 in the morning. He had not called in advance, not wanting to warn Jillian of his approach, should she be hiding there.

He tapped on the front door. There was no response, but from a side window, he saw a curtain move. He tapped again. In a minute or two, the door was opened slowly and Stella Burns peeked out at the officer.

"Oh. It's you, Deputy."

"Yes, Mrs. Burns. It's me – again – Bud Rose."

"Yes?"

"May I come in?"

"Oh. Well, I guess so. I see you didn't bring the baby."

He shook his head as she opened the door further and Bud stepped into the foyer off the living room. Stella Burns just stood there.

"I have some news that I wanted to give you – about Jillian."

"Oh, poor Jillian. My poor daughter." Tears filled her eyes.

"No, Stella. It's kind of good news. Can we go into the living room where we can sit down for a moment?"

"Sure. I guess so," and she led him toward the sofa. "You can sit there if you want."

Bud sat. She stood. "I don't want to shock you, but Jillian is alive." He was watching carefully for her reaction.

"No. No. You remember? She was drowned," and with that, Stella Burns started to cry.

"But the fact is, she didn't drown. She survived that awful accident and was living farther out on the East End."

"That's impossible." Now Stella Burns sank down on the sofa beside Bud. "She's alive? Why hasn't she called me? All this time…"

"She hasn't called, has she?"

"No. No. How could she let me go on thinking she was dead? That ungrateful girl…" Suddenly, Stella was angry.

"Jillian had her own agenda," Bud said.

"What does that mean?"

"She got a job down in Montauk and…well I don't want to go into it with you. It's enough to say that she's still in trouble."

"Oh that girl…"

"I know it's hard…disappointing. If I can help…you know Violet and I love the little girl. We're always glad to bring her to her grandma."

"I appreciate that," Stella said, sniveling.

"I do have to ask you, if you should hear…?"

"Of course, Bud. I'll let you know."

He rose. "Can you think of anywhere she might want to go?"

"Well, she always wanted to be part of the big city – you know… New York."

"Does she have friends there? I'm on my way to the city now."

"Maybe. I don't know. There was a Gracie Savage – a high school pal – she moved there a few years ago. She may be married now – different name."

"I'd best be going. We'll be in touch, Stella."

"Right, Bud. I'll show you to the door."

Stella watched as Bud glanced around. He shrugged his shoulders as raindrops began to fall, then got into his cruiser.

'He was looking for the green Chevy,' Stella thought with a smile. 'Too bad! It's in the broken down barn in the back field.'

As Bud left the driveway and turned down the street, Stella closed the door. She went to the stairwell and yelled out, "He's gone. You can come down now."

Jillian and Sasha in sweat clothes came down sheepishly from the attic space where they were staying. At the bottom of the stairs, the three embraced.

"Is it too early to have a drink?" Sasha asked.

"Well, it's five o'clock somewhere," Stella said with a laugh.

"Oh, Mom, that's old hat," joked Jillian, and the three went into the living room and toward the bar.

It didn't take long before Jillian, after downing a couple of straight shots of whiskey, started a diatribe against Bud. "That bastard…in my mother's house! So damn sanctimonious! So high and mighty."

"Jill," Stella intervened. "Bud's father to Rose Bud. He's a good man. He loves that child."

"A bastard!" Jillian exclaimed, voice shrill. "On his way to New York…to Police Headquarters yet. Well, I know where I'm going." After swallowing a third, large whisky, she slammed her glass down hard on the bar.

"That's crystal, Jillian. You'll break it," Stella admonished her.

"I'm going to collect what's due me!" she shouted at her mother.

"Jill, you're getting drunk," Stella said, moving towards the younger woman.

"That little baby girl...My Rose Bud. She's mine."

"Stop her, Sasha, for god's sake, stop her."

"She doesn't really give a damn about that baby," he mumbled, as Jillian grabbed her purse and ran out the front door. "Too late," he said casually and dropped into the nearest chair. "It's true. She couldn't care less about Rose Bud. It's all vengeance – against Bud, and particularly against his wife Violet."

Stella sank down on the couch. "Oh God," she sighed and put her hand over her eyes.

Jillian ran over the grass to the barn. It was really raining hard. She managed to pry open the heavy door of the building and clamber into the green Chevy. The keys were in the glove compartment. As she gunned the engine, she cried out loud, "Rose Bud. Mummy's coming. Hold still, baby. I'm almost there." The car moved out onto the street, after bumping out of the muddy field, and headed east toward Shore Road, Remsenburg.

It wasn't really Rose Bud she was headed for. It was Violet Rose.

Chapter Thirty-One

THE AWFUL TRUTH

Bud Rose in New York City, had planned to spend the night at the home of his cousin who had a parking garage business on the upper west side. First, he was to meet with an Inspector Flannigan of the NYPD at the office downtown near The Brooklyn Bridge, not at one of the many precincts. His mission was to bring attention – and evidence, in terms of the confessions of Martin Eldridge, former Manager of Gurney's Inn, now incarcerated in the Riverhead jail awaiting trial – to one Manhattanite, named John Grunwald.

Bud had yet to learn John Grunwald was out of the country – for an indefinite period. That fact, however, would not change the pursuit of the drug lord.

Violet was alone at home that night on Shore Road, Remsenburg, with the baby girl, Starfish.

The nights were growing colder in the autumn of that year, 1985. It was a rainy first of November, and it could be a mighty chilly month, out there on the edge of the Atlantic Ocean. Violet had the thermostat up high as she cuddled with the little child in her arms. She was even able to read some real estate notes she had made at the office, that lay next to her on the couch, the child was that quiet, that content.

The two had shared a supper of scrambled eggs, which Starfish loved, and blueberries that she stuffed in her mouth in small handfuls. It was a quiet evening under the lamplight, exactly the way a loving mother and daughter moment should be.

How quickly it was shattered! By such a small gesture did their shared serenity come to an end.

It was a tap on the door.

Violet laid the baby down on the couch on her back. She did not fuss, as Violet went to answer the front door. It was a dark day outside, although still early. Raindrops were falling. She flicked on the small porch light and saw on the stoop, the tall figure of a woman with short dark hair, one hand on hip, and a sly smile on her face.

The two women stood looking at one another, frozen. No word was spoken. Time stopped.

After what seemed like minutes, the woman said, "I'm here for Rose Bud."

"There's no Rose Bud here," Violet replied, her voice strong.

"Oh, she's here all right. And I know her daddy isn't. He's away in New York City. So you'd better let me in, Violet."

Violet started to close the door but Jillian's hand stopped it. Jillian smelled of whiskey

"Rose Bud is my baby – mine and Bud's, your precious husband. I want her back."

"Leave my house!"

"Or what? You gonna call the police?" Jillian said with a shrill laugh. "Little Miss Violet. All by herself here – alone," and Jillian forced her way into the house just as Starfish, on the couch, let out a gurgling little cry.

"There's my baby," Jillian shrieked. "There she is, my Rose Bud."

Before Jillian, arms outstretched, reached the couch, Violet ran and stood between her and the child on the cushions. Violet was shorter than Jillian, lighter, but faced her strong and protective.

"I've always hated you," Jillian snarled.

"I know."

"That's my baby." Jillian was moving one foot to the other, in a little dance. "What's the matter, Violet? Can't get pregnant? Is Bud too busy to take care of you in the sack? He sure didn't have that problem with me. Oh what sex we had!"

"Where do you think you're going to take her, Jillian?" Jillian was glaring at the smaller young woman. "I know you're on the run. She's safe here. She's happy," Violet persisted.

"But she's mine!" Jillian shouted out victoriously.

"And she's Bud's. I'm just her stepmom – but I love her as my own." Violet realized the woman was half drunk.

The two stood eyeing each other like two hostile animals – which they were – next to the prone baby.

"Think, Jillian," Violet continued. "Where are you going to keep her?"

"My mom's."

"Stella sees her. I've taken the little one there often – but your mother's arthritis is bad. In fact some days, it's hard for her to get around. And you...you're just going to drop the baby there and keep running?"

Jillian was silent.

"Is that the plan?" Violet said explosively, defiant.

Suddenly it seemed as if Jillian began to dissolve, first, tears, then she literally sank to the floor. "I'm so tired," she breathed. As she sat there with her hands over her face, Violet picked the baby up. Starfish was quiet. She took her to the crib in the large closet off the bedroom and laid her down. Starfish slept.

Returning to the living room, Violet saw that Jillian was now sitting on the couch. "Do you want a coffee?"

The woman just shook her head, then rose to her feet. She had recovered herself and stood there staring at her nemesis with a hateful gaze.

"This isn't over, Violet. Don't think for a minute it's done. It's never going to be over! I'll be back. You can count on that." With that, Jillian went to the front door, opened it and slammed it shut behind her.

Violet ran to peer out a window and saw her get into a green Chevy, pull out of the driveway, tires screeching, as the raindrops began to pelt.

She locked the door, and went quickly to the crib and picked up the baby in her arms.

The two returned to the living room. Starfish was awake, making small sweet noises as Violet held her close, murmuring sweet noises back. She realized that Jillian had not even touched the child.

"Whose baby are you really?" Violet said to the little face. "I know whose baby you are. There is no other. Starfish, you belong to me."

Violet began to sing to her, in a small, tremulous voice.

"Roses are red,

Violets are blue,

Whatever happens,

It's me and you."

Chapter Thirty-Two

A TEMPERAMENTAL SEA

The storm began by flirting with the coastline. It lapped its way almost gingerly, at first. Gradually, the pace quickened, the waves grew tall and relentless, as a full-fledged tempest hit Long Island, a force to be reckoned with.

It was that same night at the start of November. Some would later call it The Halloween Storm. Others could give it no name because it was by far the largest, the most severe of such weather events to attack the Island in decades. There were no words.

The sea, swollen, was pregnant with new life. Ice chunks, ice floes, ice, ice, ice melted at the outer edges of the planet, swelling the belly of the oceans. These were not just high tides. At first there was no rain, but then it came in huge drops. The melt though slow, was sure. The ocean spoke.

New York City was a drowned mess. Up to the storefronts, the water rose. Into the subways, the torrents poured. Bud managed the wet streets with his cruiser, though it was hard to see through the front window of the vehicle, the raindrops were dancing so hard against it.

Bud's concern was no longer John Grunwald. All he could think of – all he could care about – was Violet and Starfish – alone in the storm. But he dutifully drove downtown to police headquarters to meet Inspector Flannigan and present his evidence about John Grunwald to the local authorities.

Their meeting did not take long. Bud had brought with him a copy of

Martin Eldridge's assertions about John Grunwald. The former manager had procured emails and phone records accruing to Grunwald's former suite at The Gurney Inn. He also provided documents showing the date and time of *The Otellia's* docking at the Gurney wharf. There were even packets of heroin from Joe's Warm-Up Bar's stash.

Inspector Flannigan was impressed. "This is quite a haul, Deputy."

"Long Island is swimming in drugs. Grunwald seems to be the big honcho – certainly out there – in Montauk – where boats come and go without any sort of supervision or policing. Being a New York City resident, I'm sure gives Grunwald access to drug cartel people of every stripe."

"That's for sure. He's something of an unknown quantity but at the same time, under all sorts of suspicion," said Flannigan.

The storm was rattling the windows. It seemed stronger than ever.

"Look. I've got to get back to the Island. My wife and baby are out there alone."

"By all means, fella. Go. It'll be a nasty drive, but get going before you have darkness as well as all this rain."

"Thanks," Bud said, relieved yet worried.

"We'll take it from here. We'll contact you when we find anything and after we get a hold of Mr. Grunwald."

"I'm off," Bud said and left the headquarters swiftly.

It was a nasty drive, as Flannigan had predicted. Bud drove over The Triborough Bridge and gained the Long Island Expressway, heading east. It was pouring and traffic, in the city, and exiting out through Queens, was heavy. As he moved away from the metropolis, the number of vehicles on his side of the Expressway diminished, but the far lanes going west, were packed.

People on Long Island were trying to escape the storm, and they were driving fast and furious. Bud did not notice for a second time, Sasha's green Chevy on the other side of the Expressway, with two people inside, practically flying west toward the beacon of Manhattan.

Why would he notice? His eyes were on the slick road before him, clouded by a watery windshield that impeded his view as he cautiously drove east.

It took him almost four hours to reach Remsenburg. It was deep dark and windy and wet outside the cruiser. Trees were down, as were telephone lines, lying in puddled water, dangerous to step into.

His car approached Shore Road. The water in the street was sloughing up against his hubcaps. He could barely see.

"Thank God for headlights," he said out loud. Halfway down the road, he could see flashlights. "People," he burst out.

And then he saw her, holding the baby, Starfish, clutching her tight in her arms. There were two men with her with flashlights. One had his hand under Violet's arm, supporting her. The little group looked drenched, clothes clinging, Violet's blonde hair sticking to her head like a tight cap.

Bud's car came to a stop. It could go no farther. He got out and waded towards his wife and child and the rescuers who turned out to be firemen. Thankfully, there were no wires down on the street to electrify the puddles, a thought that never occurred to him, so eager was he to reach his wife.

"Bud," Violet screamed. "Oh, Bud, thank God you're here." He splashed toward her, grabbed hold of her, pressing against her under the pounding rain.

"The house is gone. Completely gone," she cried, tears matching the drops of water on her upturned face. "And Jillian. She came there this afternoon before the storm got so strong. She wanted Starfish," and Violet cried all the harder.

"Jillian! She left?" he said.

"Thank God, yes," replied Violet. "She's scary, Bud, real scary."

"I know. I know. She is scary." He took the baby in his arms.

"God, the baby seems to be enjoying all this water," one of the firemen said. It was true. Starfish was smiling and gurgling and licking at the wetness on her lips.

Bud lifted her up into the rain as if in homage to the storm. "That's why we call her Starfish! How she loves the sea."

"Big mistake," muttered the fireman, but Bud did not hear him.

"She's hope for the future!" Bud declared, bringing the baby down next to his wife. He turned to Violet and kissed her hard.

"The house… it's not there, anymore…only four cement stanchions sticking up in the sand. That's all that's left," Violet continued. "I wonder if Dad's place is still standing."

"Doubtful, but who knows. Those stilts," Bud responded.

He felt almost hysterical relief. He had his world – Violet and Starfish - in his arms. "There are other houses to be had, sweetheart," he exclaimed. Then with a grin, he added, "Hey, you'll find something for us. Aren't you in real estate?" Arm around her, Starfish on his hip, he slogged through the water back to his car.

She looked up at him and for the first time in hours, Violet smiled.

"There are plenty of other houses. You know that. They are just places. You, my darlings, are my home," he said as they scrambled into the car. Bud backed slowly up Shore Road and into the dark uncertainty of what lay ahead.

Starfish: The future: The encroaching sea: the arbitrary ocean: and, the swelling tide!

And, oh yes. Jillian Burns?

VIOLET

VIOLET – The Swelling Tide - the third and final volume in The Rose Trilogy, provides adventure and intrigue. Love, lust, and retribution are rampant. Still set on the East End, mysterious events and confrontations occur. The young girl, Starfish, brings hope, possibility, and surprise as the swelling tide overcomes the flat landmass that is Long Island, New York, stretching across from the Atlantic Ocean to Long Island Sound.

Printed in the United States
By Bookmasters